The Vet Upstairs

KC McCormick Çiftçi

One

O n Celia Long's first full day in Turkey, she was adopted by a cat, though she wouldn't know it until later.

It was the last thing she had expected to happen; it wasn't as if it fit with the nature of her short-term contracts and the set of rules she lived by. And that set of rules had been serving her just fine for nearly a decade.

Celia had always loved animals, from the rabbits and dogs that had played such a big role in her childhood to her friends' cats that often chose to sit on her lap when they watched movies together. No, she would have loved to have a pet—a dog, a cat, a hamster...if only she would have known that she was going to be in one place long enough to give the animal the commitment it deserved.

And that was why Celia had never bent her rules. It was also why Istanbul, from the first moment she had arrived, had seemed like paradise. Everywhere she walked, there were friendly cats on the street. They were sleeping on vacant chairs at restaurants, enjoying the sunshine next to the Blue Mosque, befriending the fishermen on the Bosphorus in hopes of sharing a fresh catch.

Celia had accepted the contract at Aslanbey Holding in part because the salary was so good—a requirement for every contract she took—but also for the opportunity to spend some time in Istanbul. She had built the city up in her mind to such expectations that the real thing couldn't possibly compete.

But compete it did. From the moment she spotted the first tiny buildings down below as her airplane neared the airport, the excitement and the romance of it all had been palpable. The blue water of the Bosphorus Strait and the Sea of Marmara, all the minarets popping up on the horizon...and was that the Hagia Sophia? Celia had first read about the historic building that had been a church, a mosque, and a museum in turns back in high school, in a World History course. There was so much to explore here, and she had six glorious months to soak up as much of the city as she could.

The apartment that Aslanbey Holding had rented for her—because that was always a requirement of her contracts these days, too—was located in Beşiktaş, walking distance from the company. Celia's days of taking taxis across town and staying in a hotel for six months were ancient history, traded in for the comfort of having her own kitchen and the peace of not having to navigate traffic in a new city. That meant the opportunities available to her were fewer, but it also meant she could keep up with her routines, could preserve the mental health that was ready to fly out the window with a lifestyle like hers.

Ten years ago, Celia had been the opposite. Every opportunity that had come her way, she'd said yes. Red eye flights, twenty-hour layovers, a bunk bed in a hostel...all of it had been an adventure. All of it had seemed fun and exciting and like she was living the dream.

Until that was no longer the case.

Until the day she had woken up in a crowded dorm room of a Paris hostel, her alarm rousing her when it was still dark out to head across town for an early meeting, at the same time that many of her fellow dorm occupants were just coming in, that she realized she'd had enough.

She wanted to sleep in a comfortable bed in a dark room with the perfect blend of silence and white noise. She wanted to wake up feeling well-rested, to drink a delicious cup of coffee, and to get dressed for the day in clothes that had hung neatly the night before inside a closet, rather than digging them from her over-packed duffel bag and giving them the sniff test before heading out. She wanted a relaxed, leisurely journey to work and a sleep schedule that worked with her body rather than against it.

And so, like that, she had traded in her short-term contracts and travel-centric lifestyle for longer commitments. No longer was she adjusting to a new time zone every few days; now, she was staying put long enough to recognize faces at the coffee shop and sometimes, even, to have her coffee order remembered before she could place it.

This lifestyle had suited Celia so well that it was rare that she entertained a fantasy of staying put. Of putting down roots altogether and trading in her suitcase for a bookcase or some other piece of furniture. Sure, there were moments when she missed her family and friends back in

St. Louis, but those usually abated with a visit back for a holiday—or at least for her quarterly check-in.

No, this is the dream. She reminded herself of that truth as she unpacked her suitcase, hanging her business casual attire in a new wardrobe for the umpteenth time. *It's not like it's the third time I've unpacked this month. It's only the second time this year. And it's exciting! Who doesn't like a fresh start?*

Once the suitcase was tucked away under Celia's bed—it was better if it was out of sight, not reminding her of her eventual departure but giving her at least the illusion that she *lived* somewhere—she took off in search of food. If experience had taught her anything, it was that spending her first night in a new city at home on the couch was a recipe for longing. Whether it was longing for home, longing for something—anything—familiar, or simply questioning all her life choices that had led her to that moment, it wasn't the way she wanted to spend her first night in Istanbul.

Instead, she walked. She walked to see the sights, she walked to find the most delicious food her nose could sniff out, and she walked away from any feelings that were not welcome on this most exciting night of her new adventure. As a last stop before returning to her apartment, she walked up and down the aisles of a grocery store, filling her cart with everything that caught her eye. While debating between two different varieties of yogurt, she ended up with both of them in her cart. After all, what could be worse than making the wrong choice?

"No, that's ridiculous," she muttered to herself, as she shoved one pot of yogurt back onto the refrigerated shelf.

"At least in the world of yogurt, making the wrong choice isn't *that* big a deal. Maybe just this once it's okay *not* to try to have it all." She rolled her eyes at her own ridiculousness, before venturing in search of fruit to put in her yogurt, and a similar debate over which one was the "right" choice, if her past behavior was an accurate predictor of her future actions. It wasn't as if she couldn't make a different choice on her next trip to the grocery store, either.

She sat on her couch when she returned to the new apartment that didn't yet feel like "home," with a small bowl of yogurt that she had cut a peach into. Staring at the wall—the remote for the TV was out of reach, and the exhaustion of the day had caught up to her—she nodded a few times. "Not bad," she said, as she scooped another slice of peach and a dollop of rich, creamy yogurt onto her spoon. "Not bad at all." She might be feeling the tiniest bit homesick, might even be doubting her decision to continue starting over again in new cities...but at least she could put together a damn fine snack.

Two

That first day at Aslanbey Holding had gone like most of Celia's first days as an efficiency consultant did—a tour of the premises, introductions to everyone she would be working with, and then a good portion of the day spent going over standard operating procedures and getting the lay of the land.

She had enjoyed unexpected company at lunch when Ayla, the assistant to the CEO, had joined her in the breakroom. While Celia preferred not to make personal connections—it would be the pinnacle of awkwardness if she befriended someone on the first day that she ended up having to let go later—it was impossible to deny Ayla. The younger woman had been so eager to speak English, to offer advice about the neighborhood, and even to share her lunch that before Celia knew it, she found her regular professional boundaries dissolving, only barely managing to stop herself from telling Ayla about the cocktail of feelings that had visited her the night before. She excused herself with a polite smile and a silent admonishment to get her act together before her next shared meal with Ayla.

As was also typical for Celia's first day at a new contract, she left promptly at the end of the workday. This served two functions: first, she was often adjusting to a new time zone on that day and unable to keep her exhaustion from poking through her professional façade, and secondly, it was important to set clear expectations from the jump. While Celia had no problem with staying late to work on important projects—what else was she going to do in the evenings, anyway?—doing so on the first day might give the wrong impression and set the expectation that staying late was the norm. Both for herself and for the other employees, she didn't want that.

That's how she ended up arriving back at her Beşiktaş apartment just after five thirty on a Wednesday afternoon, and just in time to meet the cat that would adopt her. As she walked up to the building, she heard an insistent meow. Something about it made her stop in her tracks and turn in a slow circle to find the source. The meow was so repetitive, so unwavering that she feared she would find a cat in distress, or worse, injured.

But as she turned, there was nothing. Not a cat to be found, not on the ground near her feet, not on the low brick wall surrounding the apartment complex, not...

Oh. There you are. Celia's eyes drifted just above her eye line to a tree at the far back corner of the garden surrounding the apartment building. And sure enough, there on the lowest branch—which was still above the top of Celia's head—was the source of the noise.

A small tabby cat was perched on the branch, eyes intent on Celia as it meowed repeatedly at her.

Celia approached, cautious. "Are you stuck in the tree?" she asked the cat. "I'm not a firefighter, you know. And I think if I climb up there to try to get you, we're both going to end up hurt."

As if the cat understood what she had said, it stood up, meowed three more times, and then walked to the trunk of the tree, turned around, and lowered itself backwards, and reverse climbed down to the ground.

"Wow. I...did not know you could do that," said Celia. "Of course, we just met, so there's a lot I don't know about you."

The cat twined itself around Celia's legs, now adding a rumbling purr underneath its incessant meows. Celia reached down to pet the cat, but before she could even get her hand down to the level of its head, the cat gave a small jump with its front legs to meet her hand in the air, doing half the work of petting itself, no help needed.

A chuckle bubbled out of Celia's throat. "Oh, you are cute. Do you live around here? Are you hungry?" She looked around the garden, but she saw no signs that the cat lived there or was cared for there regularly. There were no dishes for food or water, no cat beds or dog houses. She had seen all of those things out on the surrounding streets while out for walks, and wondered if she should take the initiative on setting that up here.

She started to walk towards the entrance of the building, planning to go inside, drop off her things, and then head to the store to find some cat food for her new friend. But as she took her first steps, one problem became apparent: the cat was not going to let Celia out of its sight. With every step, it continued to rub against her calves, first the outside of one leg, then the inside of the other, until the two of them had arrived at the door like they were doing some kind of (very slow) three-legged race.

A six-legged race, more like, Celia thought to herself.

"Okay, then...er...Cat? Sorry, I don't know if you've got a name. But, er...I'm going to need to go inside, you see. If you want me to get you some food, I mean...then I need to go in that door first. And you need to stay out here. Oh no! I said stay out here, Cat!" While she had been talking, Celia had opened the door and made an attempt to sneak inside. But despite the fact that she had only opened the door just as wide as she needed to in order to squeeze through—and, in fact, not quite wide enough, as she'd banged the tip of her nose on it in her haste—the cat had made it inside and bolted up the stairs before Celia could stop her.

"Where are you?" She hissed the words, not wanting to alert the rest of the building's tenants that there was an errant cat wandering the hallways. Were pets even allowed in this building? She couldn't remember hearing any rules about that, but it wasn't as if she had asked. Considering that she didn't travel with a pet of her own, she didn't much care if other people had their own animals around. It might even be nice to run into a friendly dog in the hallway to pat on the head.

Celia walked up the stairs to her third-floor apartment, and she didn't see the cat on the way up. Each floor had just two apartments on it, so it was unlikely that she had missed spotting the cat on one of the lower floors. It had to be at the level of her apartment or higher. She groaned to herself as she imagined trudging up all the stairs to catch the cat at the top of the building. If there was a way to get access to the roof, she had a feeling it might even be all the way up there.

She turned the corner of the landing between the second and third floor, her front door coming into view. Her suspicions about the cat's preference for extreme heights had proven to be incorrect, as the cat was currently sniffing Celia's shoes outside her apartment.

From the first time that she had entered the building, Celia had noted that all the other tenants kept their shoes outside their apartments, stashed in front of their doors. In fact, when her liaison at Aslanbey Holding had first showed her the apartment, both of them had followed suit and slipped their shoes off before doing the walkthrough.

Not only did it help keep dirt from the streets and sidewalks from getting tracked inside, but apparently it also helped stray cats identify their new friends by their smell. At Celia's approach, the cat looked up from the shoe it had been sniffing, and meowed in greeting.

"Geez, you were quick up those stairs, Cat." Celia shook her head. "I don't know what to tell you, but you can't come into my apartment. That's for sure. There's no cat food in there, no litter box...and I'm only here for six months. If you come inside now, what are you going to do when I leave? Hmm?"

The cat chirped its response, approaching Celia as she slipped her shoes off and rubbing against her legs in the process. How this animal had gotten this attached to her—and become this insistent about giving its affection to her and her alone—was a mystery to her.

As Celia unlocked the door, she braced herself to dart inside without letting the cat in with her. She would use her briefcase as a barricade and make a quick entrance—what could go wrong?

This time, she actually did make it through the door without a cat surprising her on the other side. As she closed the door behind her, she heard the meows get more insistent. The cat's frustration at being abandoned in the hallway was apparent, and Celia shook her head at it. "We just met!" She was talking to herself again. "This is way too much and way too soon. If that cat is trying to get adopted, it's like dating. You don't try to move in with each other on the first date. Or scratch that, we don't even know each other's names yet, so I don't think this could even be considered a first date!"

Celia left her briefcase in the kitchen, then went into her bedroom to change into some more comfortable, more casual clothes. She had been dressed for meetings today, and the sooner she could take off her stockings, her button-down blouse, and her pencil skirt, the better. Jeans and a t-shirt would be much more comfortable, and have much lower stakes for whatever cat wrangling she was about to do.

Her bedroom was the furthest room from the apartment's entrance, and when she was inside it, she could no longer hear any meows out in the hallway. "Maybe it went away," she mumbled to herself. "In that case, I can at least let it back outside. I don't think my neighbors will like me too much if I'm the reason a cat starts pooping on the stairs."

That was all the reminder she needed that this errand was time-sensitive. Pausing in the kitchen to grab an apple,

Celia shoved her wallet and keys in her pocket and opened the door...

...and immediately had to block one striped paw from bolting inside.

"Cat!" she exclaimed. "You're still here." Celia was grinning now. As much as she had entertained the possibility that the cat had given up on her, she was more than a little pleased to find that hadn't been the case. There was something about an animal camping outside her door that made her feel...chosen. It wasn't a feeling she got to experience often in her personal life—it ran completely counter to the nature of her job and lifestyle, packing up and starting over again every six months—and she was surprised to discover that she'd missed it this much.

The cat followed Celia down the stairs, meowing all the way as if it were telling her all the things that had happened while she'd been at work that day. Celia, for her part, munched on her apple and made soft sounds back to the cat. If any of her neighbors were listening at their doors, she didn't want them to think she was actually talking to a cat...but she also didn't want to be rude to her new little friend.

At the bottom of the stairs, she opened the door, and the cat trotted out into the garden in front of her, still close enough to touch if she leaned down. Celia stopped where she stood and cocked her head to the side, peering down at the cat. "I've got to call you something. *Cat* just won't do...but I don't know if you already have a name." She shrugged. "Or even if you already have a human that you live with! But if that's the case, what if we just have a little secret between us? Even if you live with someone and they already named you Fluffy or something like that, it could be like your nickname. My name for you." Celia paused to think. Not only had she never named another living being, but she'd never named another living being in a different language. Should the cat have a Turkish name or an English name? Or what about something that sounded good in both languages? It would help if she knew more than basic pleasantries in Turkish (so far she had just about mastered "hello" and "thank you," so she had a long way to go).

Hoping that the right name would find its way to her with a minimum of effort on her part, Celia stopped in the garden to let the cat know about her plans. "You stay here," she told it. "I'm going to go find some food for you, but stay in the garden, okay? There are a lot of cars on the street out there, and I want you to be safe." The cat meowed back at her, followed her through the garden for a bit, but stopped at the gate and remained inside, as if it had understood her request.

Celia returned to the apartment building twenty minutes later with a bag of cat food, a bottle of water, and two bowls. She had felt ridiculous buying bottled water for a cat when she had an actual water source inside her apartment...until she remembered what had happened the last time she had opened the door while the cat was around. Better to spend some extra liras on a bottle of water than to be chasing a cat up and down the stairs for the rest of the evening.

As she arranged the bowls, filling one with water and one with dry cat food, the cat purred with appreciation at her feet, rubbing its head against her hand while she worked. Once the cat was eating, Celia crouched down next to it, scratching its back and speaking softly while the cat ate and purred, the most content animal within at least the district, if not all of Istanbul.

Aware of the sound of approaching steps, Celia looked up. She hadn't been staying in the building long enough to meet any of her neighbors yet, but this one...well, she definitely would have recognized this one if she'd met him before. The man walking towards her was tall and muscular, dressed casually but clearly with an eye for style in dark denim, a fitted black t-shirt, and a blue cardigan. He was wearing sunglasses in the late afternoon, but even without a clear view of his eyes, she was stunned by his handsome face. His bone structure, artfully messy hair—which looked as if he'd run his hands through it multiple times throughout the day, rather than spending his morning carefully styling it—and the five o'clock shadow of stubble covering his jawline were all the stuff of fashion magazines and expensive photo shoots.

She briefly wondered to herself if he was someone famous. Was she supposed to know him from somewhere? She didn't watch any Turkish TV shows—not yet, at least—but she wouldn't have been half surprised to see this man gracing one of them with his larger-than-life presence.

His hands were full of grocery bags, and Celia bolted to her feet to open the door for him in an act of neighborly kindness. After all, it *was* weird that she was camped out in front of the door, wasn't it? And stepping in as a doorwoman of sorts might at least take some attention away from what she was doing. She didn't even know if the apartment building had a rule about pets, after all, and they might not appreciate her actions, which were likely going to coax this friendly stray cat to stick around.

So she pulled the door open and ducked her head as the man approached, his steps slowing as he got closer. He smiled, first at her and then at the cat, coming to a stop. "*Merhaba*," he greeted her, switching to English at her blank expression. "Hello," he said then. "It looks like you've made a friend."

She gave him a sheepish smile back. "I guess so. And I wasn't even trying!" She tipped her head towards the door, subtly letting him know that he could continue inside, that he didn't need to feel obligated to stand here with her and watch a cat eat. "Have a good evening!"

"You, too." He leaned down towards the cat, who stopped eating to look up at him with a single chirp-like meow. "*Afiyet olsun, Minnoş*. You have a good evening too. Maybe let the nice lady go inside and get some rest, hmm?"

Celia smiled and nodded, letting the door close gently behind him once he was inside. "Who was that?" she whispered, partly to herself and partly to the cat. "Friend of yours?" That was directed to the cat, who was once again whiskers-deep in its food bowl.

"Fine, then. You keep your secrets." Celia gave the cat one last stroke along the back, its spine lifting up involuntarily to meet her hand. "See you later."

Three

Celia's evening was spent in front of her computer, one necessary evil of her work status. Even if she made a point of leaving the office on time, that didn't mean her evenings belonged to herself. If she were the kind of person who worked somewhere longer than six months, she would insist on leaving work at work and spending her evenings relaxing and watching movies...but with the territory of exciting new locations and new professional challenges around every corner came a certain lack of work-life balance.

That was another tug she felt when she thought about settling down someday. What would it be like if she had a partner waiting for her at home, someone to shoot frustrated glances her way or sigh loudly when she picked up her phone at the dinner table? Even more, what would it be like to be someone who *didn't* spend her evenings tethered to her work by phone and email? As it was, she barely had time to entertain that possibility. From first waking to falling asleep in front of a screen most nights, she always had something to occupy her thoughts.

That was why companies like Aslanbey Holding brought her in, after all. When they had gotten themselves into a bind, when systems and operations were such a mess that money was being wasted and work wasn't getting done properly, Celia Long was a fixer. And there was nothing she loved more than a good puzzle that needed to be solved.

The information gathering stage was always a treat. She pored over all the information provided to her, the human resources handbooks and employee profiles, the standard operating procedures, the descriptions of responsibilities that each employee handled, along with the company's mission statement and values. It felt similar to reading a mystery novel, in that Celia prided herself on being able to figure out the mystery before it was revealed. On noticing the subtle foreshadowing and minor hints that others might overlook, that might make them gasp in shock, "Wow, I didn't see that coming!"

Because, more often than not, Celia *did* see it coming, both in the novels and in her professional life. Something would catch her eye and alert her to an employee, a team, a specific workflow where something was missing. Unaccounted for. Overlooked by everyone but her. And then the second game would begin. The game where she had to put all the pieces back together but make them all fit this time.

It was thrilling. She knew it might not be considered thrilling—or even attention-worthy—to most people, but it was an actual dream job for Celia. It was exciting enough to almost make her forget about the homesickness that knocked on the edge of her consciousness on a night like this, when she was still finding her footing in a new city. If she couldn't be Sherlock Holmes or Hercule Poirot, at least she could solve these mysteries of her own. Take them apart and put them back together again, the full picture coming into focus only when she had stepped back at the end to take it all in.

And that's what she was thinking about as she began to pore over the Aslanbey Holding files that evening, a highlighter in one hand, a stack of sticky notes beside her, and a mug full of herbal tea at her side. It's what she was preparing to dive into when she heard the distinct sound outside her apartment door.

The meow was quiet, tentative. But it was there, and it was familiar. And before she even knew why, Celia was getting to her feet and moving towards it, a smile spreading across her face.

Four

Celia hadn't planned on having a roommate in Istanbul, and yet there she was, setting up a blanket on the couch, making a nice little nest for the cat—who she had decided to call Badem, after seeing the word on a packet of almonds in her kitchen—to sleep in.

"I must be out of my mind," she mumbled to herself. "A strange animal, sleeping in my home? This *can't* be normal behavior."

It had started innocently enough. After Badem had meowed by her door, Celia had let her inside and Badem had jumped right up on the couch like she lived there. She was comfortable enough in the apartment that Celia had to wonder if she had lived there before. If, perhaps, the previous tenant had left her behind when they had moved out. But Badem snuggling up on the couch next to her, purring, had quickly turned into Badem curled into a ball at the opposite end of the couch, sleeping soundly while Celia attempted to return to her work.

When she had gotten up to get herself ready for bed, Badem hadn't moved an inch by the time she returned from brushing her teeth, and that's when Celia began to think that kicking this little visitor of hers out for the night just might be cruel and unusual. She found the spare blanket in the bedroom and placed it on the couch, an invitation for Badem to make herself (even more) comfortable should the need arise.

There was nothing on the counter for Badem to get into if she woke up in the middle of the night, which just left the concern about the lack of a litter box. Celia knew enough about cats to know that they were clean animals, unlikely to make a mess unless the need was dire. And at that point, Celia was both too tired to venture out in search of cat litter and too soft-hearted to send Badem back down the stairs.

"Here's hoping for the best then," Celia said as she reached down to give Badem a few goodnight strokes. A soft murmur from Badem acknowledged the touch, but her eyes remained closed, her breathing deep. "If you need to go to the bathroom, wake me up, okay?"

Celia shook her head at herself as she switched off the lights and made her way to her bedroom. "This will at least make a great story later, however it turns out. Hopefully, it's a cute story, and not the story of how I woke up to an apartment covered in cat crap and with everything I own destroyed."

She tossed and turned as soon as she was in her bed, jet lag throwing her body into a mix of confusion and exhaustion that needed rest and brain stimulation simultaneously. Closing her eyes only made her mind race with thoughts, while keeping them open was a near impossibility.

Celia was squeezing her eyes closed and tensing every muscle in her body—that was supposed to make the relaxation even sweeter, wasn't it?—when she heard soft footsteps padding down the hallway. A quiet chirp announced Badem's presence a moment before a cat-shaped shadow appeared on the bed next to Celia, a soft indentation in the mattress. Celia turned onto her side and watched in the near darkness as Badem purred and rubbed her head against the outline of Celia's knees. When she made her way up to Celia's face, she curled up next to her, a little spoon nestling in next to Celia's big spoon, her little cat head finding a perfect fit in the crook of Celia's arm.

And that's how Celia finally fell asleep.

...and it's how Celia woke up the next morning, too. She looked down at the small, fuzzy sleeping form next to her, an unfamiliar pang in her chest as she sat up and Badem came back to consciousness. "Good morning," she greeted her little friend, who woke up with her little cat motor revving at full capacity, purrs that likely could be heard from the next apartment. "You are a great sleeping buddy, Badem. I haven't slept that well in a long time."

Badem meowed in response and yawned, standing up to stretch. The yawn was contagious, and Celia gave a full body stretch as well before putting her feet down on the floor beside the bed.

"What first?" she asked the cat. "Cat food for you or coffee for me?" She groaned as she remembered that she had left the bag of cat food outside the apartment's door. It had seemed like such a good idea at the time, confident as she was that she would continue to feed Badem regularly outside the apartment, not that she would let her inside and allow her to sleep in her bed.

Celia started the kettle, then wrapped herself in a cardigan to make her way downstairs to the cat food. Was she really going to bring everything back up to her apartment? Surely, Badem would be more comfortable and happier with free rein of the apartment's garden and trees than cooped up inside.

As if in answer to that question, the cat followed Celia to the door and slipped outside with her. Only, when Celia made it to the landing of the stairs, she realized Badem wasn't with her. "Weird," she mumbled. "Maybe she rushed past me and I didn't see. Poor thing is probably hungry." But when she got down the stairs, the cat wasn't there either.

Celia shook her head and turned, trudging back up the stairs. It was pointless to go outside and fill the food and water dishes there if her feline friend wouldn't be around to appreciate it. But where had she wandered off to...?

She walked up the stairs, eagle eyes searching for any places—a shelf full of shoes, perhaps—where the cat could be hiding. But by the time she had arrived in front of her door, there had been no sign of Badem. Not even a whisker.

Celia sighed as she trudged up the next flight of stairs. "It's way too early for this. You couldn't have at least let me drink my coffee before playing a game of hide and seek?"

As she turned the next corner and arrived at the fourth floor, there was the cause of her early morning scavenger hunt—none other than the very same cat who had shared her bed the night before. Only now, she was standing on her hind legs, scratching at the door of an unfamiliar apartment. As Celia approached, Badem didn't stop her desperate entreaty to get the attention of the resident of the apartment, either. If anything, it was as if she had been trying to be discreet, to not get Celia's attention, and now that her cover had been blown, she began to meow.

It was a meow Celia hadn't heard yet. Not the cute, petite meow of a cat who was trying to endear itself to a new human or the greeting of a friend. This was bordering on a howl, more reminiscent of an alarm than a greeting, and Celia's eyes widened in shock and horror.

The cat was going to wake up the entire building if she didn't do something about it. If anyone else was still sleeping through this, that was a borderline miracle, but whoever was inside that apartment was surely tromping towards the door at that very moment, ready to whip it open and scold the naughty animal—

And in that moment, as if the action had been created by her thoughts, the door did, in fact, fly open.

But the expression of the person on the other side, well...it was nothing like Celia had imagined. Had feared. No, the man who opened the door was beaming from ear to ear, eyes trained on Badem like she was a sailor returning from months at sea, not a stray animal begging for a scrap of food.

As the man—Celia realized now, with a different kind of horror, that it was the same handsome man she had seen in the garden yesterday, when she had awkwardly held the door open—bent down to pet the cat's head, she tried to disappear. To moonwalk back down the stairs, moving so slowly and stealthily that she just might escape undetected.

But it wasn't meant to be, not if Badem had anything to say about it.

By the time Celia had taken her first step backwards, her head nearly lowering out of the man's eyeline, she saw with shock that he had picked the cat up and was cradling her in both of his arms, kissing her on the top of her head while speaking to her like she was a baby. She couldn't hear what he was saying, and she guessed she wouldn't be able to understand it if she could, but it was such an intimate sight and the affection between the two beings was so obvious that Celia was simultaneously drawn closer and propelled away. Like she shouldn't be intruding on this precious moment, but at the same time, who in their right mind could see a movie star-handsome man cuddle with a cat like he was posing for a calendar and not want to insert herself into the scene?

And that's how Celia ended up frozen in place as the cat took that precise moment to turn her face in her direction and meow loudly, directing the man's attention right where she didn't want it.

Because there she was, in her pajamas and cardigan, unwashed face and unbrushed hair, harried from the wild goose chase Badem had sent her on, in the exact opposite state in which she would typically wish to encounter an attractive member of the opposite sex. If their encounter in the garden yesterday had been awkward, then this would take it to a whole new level. This took that weird little dance they'd done and cranked it up to eleven. Now, there was bedhead and morning breath and—she wrapped her cardigan around herself a little more snugly at the realization—braless pajamas. This was fifth date level vulnerability, at the very least, and here she was giving it out for free before they'd even exchanged names.

"Er...hi," she said, realizing the only thing that made this all worse was the fact that she was just staring, open-mouthed, with no words coming out. "I was...just, uh...looking for the cat. But you found her. So. Yeah." She turned on her heel, waving with a toothy and strained grin over her shoulder as she took a step down the stairs. "See you both later then."

"Hold on a moment." The man's deep voice cut through her discomfort. "You were looking for Minnoş? She just came to say hello. You should take her with you."

Celia turned back in time to see him place the cat on the ground. She raised up on her back legs to rub her head on the man's knee, then trotted towards Celia and back down the stairs.

"How...?" Celia was at a loss for words. "How did you know? And why did she come up here? Is that your cat?" A beat passed as a thought occurred, horrifying Celia. "Did I *steal* your cat last night?"

The man threw his head back with laughter, a grin spreading across his face. "She probably came up to say hello and steal a bit of my breakfast. Minnoş has a lot of friends in the building, and she's always trying to sneak inside. I don't think she's anyone's cat, but I get the feeling she would like to be. If you want to adopt her, I think she'd be a very happy lady."

"Ah. Well, okay then. That's good to know." Celia felt an upside down smile form on her face. "She's very sweet. Makes me wish I was staying longer, so I could give her the home she's looking for."

"Oh?" His expression changed to match hers. "You're not here long term? That's too bad, then. For Minnoş, I mean."

Celia nodded. "I'll see what I can do for her, at least. If she can't be my cat, at least I can make sure she gets a vet check-up. If she's going to be visiting my apartment and sleeping there, the least I can do is make sure she doesn't have fleas or anything like that. Not a bad idea to see about vaccinations, spaying, the usual. Whether she's staying with me or not, she should be healthy."

His forehead creased in thought, no doubt processing just how quickly Celia had gone from looking for a strange cat to making an action plan for its medical care. "That's true." He took a step towards her, holding out his hand. "My name is Enes, by the way. It's nice to meet you."

"Celia," she said with a quick squeeze of his hand. "I should get ready for work. Do you happen to know, by any chance, if there's a vet nearby? Preferably someone who will be open in the evening once I'm back from work and can take...er...Minnoş? Was that her name?"

Enes grinned. "That's what I call her, but it doesn't mean you have to name her that. It's more like a nickname, anyway. And yes, there's a vet's office just a few blocks away. You know the mosque just up the road?" He pointed in the direction Celia walked to her office, and she nodded. "If you turn left there, just keep going straight. It's on the opposite side of the street, but you can't miss it."

"Got it. Thank you, Enes. Have a nice day." Celia gave a feeble wave and then continued down the stairs, finding Badem waiting on the landing below to lead her all the way down to the building's entrance and outside. After she had given the cat fresh food and water and a few extra scratches under the chin, she slipped back into the building and up to her apartment to get ready for the day.

As she got dressed in her business casual attire and put on her standard work makeup look, Celia shook her head at herself in the mirror. "You can look pretty hot when you want to, you know that, right? So why is it that every time you've seen this Enes man, you've managed to be either the most socially awkward version of yourself or the most un-washed you can possibly be?" She raised an eyebrow, but her reflection didn't have anything to say in response. "Do better," she chided herself. "No more opening the door to your apartment unless you're looking your best and ready to have a sparks-flying moment with the cute neighbor. Not even if you're just sneaking downstairs really quickly to feed Badem. Goodness knows that cat is going to keep making the two of you cross paths, and if you let her, she'll make sure you're good and thoroughly embarrassed every single time. But you can't let that happen. You got that?"

A chuckle escaped from Celia's lips. At least when Badem had been in the apartment with her, she'd been talking to another living being, even if that being was a cat and even if there was a very good chance that, if Badem were suddenly going to receive the gift of speech and talk like a human, she would speak Turkish rather than English. But without the cat around, Celia was just talking to herself. And she'd gotten a little too comfortable talking to herself in the years she'd been working on these short-term con-tracts. It was either that or not talking to anyone. If she'd wanted to video chat with someone back home, the time difference would have been punishing for one of them and a great way to get her old friends and roommates to block her phone number.

Not that there was anything wrong with talking to herself. Celia had learned early on in the game of living alone and moving countries a couple of times a year that she had to enjoy her own company. Laugh at her own jokes. Be her own best friend. And part of being her own best friend was talking herself through awkward and weird and uncomfortable situations.

Now, it was true that a best friend who *didn't* live inside her own head might be a little more generous of spirit. If she had a best friend who told her she was a weirdo or a freak or a loser, she wouldn't keep that person around long enough for them to finish their sentence. She needed to work on not talking to herself like a crappy friend would, but like a kind and loving friend would. The friend who offered unconditional support and reassurance, rather than unwanted—and often unjustified—criticism and harsh critique.

She left for the day soon after, finding Badem napping in the morning sun in the garden. Celia promised to pick up some cat treats on her way home and asked the cat to, in return, be ready and available for a little trip to the vet when she got back.

"If you're going to be sleeping in my apartment—in my bed, no less—we've got to take care of a few things. Okay?" She rubbed Badem's back, the animal rolling over to expose her belly and get some scratches there, too. "That looks like an agreement to me, even if it's not *exactly* how we make a deal at work." Her eyes flicked to her watch.

"Speaking of which, I've gotta go. Catch you later, my kitty friend."

Five

As tended to happen—and yet she was surprised by it every time—Celia's second day on the new contract was better than the first. She knew a bit more about how things worked (or at least where the bathroom and coffee machine were), and there were a few more friendly faces checking in with her. Once again, Ayla joined her for lunch, her company quickly growing on Celia. If the first day sometimes made her wish she had taken a different job or stayed at home this time around, the second day reminded her why she had gotten into this field in the first place.

Because she loved getting to know new businesses, and she loved meeting new people along the way. Sure, those people were often wary of her, mistakenly believing that she was only there to choose who was going to get fired next. But in making the businesses more effective, the people working there got to change their work up, too. A job that had been confusing or monotonous reflected a problem, and once that problem was unraveled, the job often became more interesting, the employee more invested. That led the upper management team to be more appreciative of their workforce, which typically translated into bonuses and benefits that trickled down to their employees.

The second day was also less exhausting than the first, thanks in part to a solid night of rest, abating the effects of jet lag ever so slightly. So when Celia returned to her apartment building at the end of the day to be greeted by Badem and reminded of their impending date with the vet, she just smiled. It would be nice to walk around a bit, see a new part of the neighborhood. And, of course, to get Badem ready for life on the inside.

On her walk home from the office, Celia had ducked into a pet shop to pick up a cat carrier for the journey to the vet's office. As friendly as Badem was, there was a chance she would have followed Celia all the way there on her own. But with the cars on the street and plenty of other cats milling around, it might not be the safest, and she didn't want to take that chance.

And so, once she had dropped her things off inside and changed into jeans and a t-shirt, Celia went back downstairs, cat carrier and treats in hand. Badem was easily enticed inside the carrier, thanks in part to the treats, but even without them, she had seemed more than willing to follow Celia's directions. Only when she was inside the carrier with the door closed, when Celia picked it up and began walking in the direction Enes had told her that morning...only then did a few wary meows begin to emanate from the carrier.

"It's okay, Badem girl. We're just going to the vet's office for a little check-up and we'll be back home again before you know it."

She walked by the mosque, the same one from which she had heard the call to prayer in the early hours this morning. It had crept into her dreams, her consciousness weaving it into whatever storyline she had been invested in that was long since forgotten. From previous contracts where she'd lived near schools with musical interludes between classes or churches with regular ringing of bells, she knew she would get used to the sound of the call to prayer. That at some point it wouldn't wake her up at all and she might not even hear it. But it had been comforting, somehow, this morning. A very tangible reminder that even if it was dark out and quiet, that she wasn't alone. The whole neighborhood, the whole city, was just waiting to spring to life.

One more turn, and there it was. Celia spotted the small veterinarian's office across the street, checked that there was no traffic coming, and jogged across, Badem meowing a little more urgently at her increased pace.

A bell rang as she pushed open the door, but the waiting room was empty. Celia stood there, lifting the cat carrier up to eye level, as she waited for someone to hear the bell and come check on her. Someone *must* be here, right?

As she murmured softly to Badem and debated leaving to try again another day, quick footsteps approached from the hallway behind the reception desk.

"*Hoş geldiniz!*" The voice welcoming her into the office came from a petite, gray-haired woman who looked to be in her early sixties. Her warm smile and kind eyes trained on Celia as she continued to speak, though Celia's Turkish comprehension had been maxed out after her initial "welcome."

Celia bit her lip apologetically. "Sorry," she said. "Do you speak English?" The woman smiled and nodded, and Celia sighed out a deep exhale. "Oh, good. It's just...I barely know how to order coffee in Turkish, so talking about animal health things would just be..."

"Very difficult, I know." The woman's eyes were crinkling in the corner as she searched Celia's face like it contained the answers as to what she was doing there. "How can we help you today? What brings you here?" She ducked down to peer into the cat carrier, which was back down by Celia's side now. "Who is this?"

"This is Badem." Celia lifted the carrier again, to the level of the woman's eyes. "I just moved here, and I just met her yesterday. She's really friendly, and she's really insistent that she wants to come live inside. I just...well, I wanted to make sure she had all the medical things taken care of that she needed. Immunizations, spaying, that kind of thing."

"Okay, that's great. Let's take her back to the examination room, then. The vet will come look at her shortly. He's just finishing up with another patient."

"Oh. Sure." Celia's smile faltered for a moment in her confusion as she began to follow the woman down the hallway. "I thought you were the vet. I'm sorry about that."

The woman looked back at her over her shoulder with a smile and a dismissive wave. "Don't be sorry. I am here a lot, helping out, so I do know a lot of things and am always happy to meet a new patient."

"You don't work here?" This was getting more confusing by the minute.

The woman shook her head. "My son is the vet, and I don't have as much to do these days now that I'm retired. I like to come here and help out."

"Ah, I see. That's really wonderful of—"

But her next words were cut off as they entered the examination room to find three shining examination tables, one with a kitten on it who was being attended to by a man with a *very* familiar face. And considering how long Celia had been in Istanbul, there weren't many familiar faces around at all outside of the office.

"It's you." She greeted Enes with an incredulous laugh, setting the cat carrier down to fold her arms over her chest. "You told me where the vet's office was, but you neglected to mention that *you* were the vet."

Enes straightened up, smiling at her as he scratched the frustrated kitten in front of him behind the ear and then expertly scooted it back into its carrier. "That's true. Can you forgive me for trying to drum up a little business, though? It's not as if there's another vet's office that's closer."

Celia snorted, an indelicate laugh that snuck out before she could stop it. "I don't begrudge you marketing your business at all. I just find it hilarious and bizarre that you left out the teeny tiny detail that you're a vet."

Enes picked up the carrier with the kitten in it, handing it off to his assistant—his *mom*, Celia reminded herself—who carried it out of the room, back to the waiting room where they had met. When they were alone, Enes bent down in front of the carrier with Badem in it, who meowed at the sight of him, poking one small paw through the bars of the cage.

"You actually brought her in," said Enes. He lifted the carrier up to the examination table, opening the door to let Badem out and onto the shiny surface.

"Of course." Celia's eyes widened. "Did you think I wouldn't?"

Enes shrugged. "You're not the first person to take an interest in her. Ever since she was a kitten, she's been campaigning to get someone in that building to take her inside. The last person who lived in your apartment even brought her in for a while."

Celia nodded, a vague feeling of deflation coming over her. "That makes sense. That's probably why she seemed so familiar with it. Why she chose me in the first place."

"Maybe. It might be about you too, though. Cats have a way of sensing people who will be good to them. I suspect it was that more than the apartment itself. As I remember, there was plenty of drama, raised voices and things like that, coming from that apartment before you moved in. I don't think an animal would gravitate to a place like that just because it was familiar. But I saw you with her. You fed her, gave her water...why wouldn't she want to come inside and be your friend?"

"I guess so." Celia paused, reflecting on the short time she had already known Badem. "I didn't think it would happen that quickly, not at all. I fed her yesterday because she seemed hungry and like she wanted attention. The way she wanted to move in together so quickly...that's like something straight out of a romance novel. Love at first sight, instalove, whatever you want to call it." She scoffed.

"I guess it's possible that something like that exists in *this* context."

Enes raised an eyebrow at her. "A skeptic about love at first sight? How original." He held up a hand in protest before she could say anything, his other hand holding Badem in place on the table. "I'm just teasing. For humans, it's probably just attraction at first sight, you're right." He gestured down to Badem, who had flipped onto her back, exposing her belly to both of them. "But how could anyone not love *this* at just one look?"

Celia reached down to rub the belly—who could resist?—at the same time that Enes apparently had the same thought. Their hands brushed against each other's, and she pulled away, moving hers to Badem's head while leaving him sole custody of the furry belly. "You'd have to be a monster," she admitted. "There's no other explanation."

Six

The vet visit didn't last long. Badem needed a few routine immunizations, but seemed to be in perfect health otherwise. Enes advised, however, that if Celia wanted to, it would be wise to have her spayed.

Celia hesitated for just a moment. "Is that definitely necessary?" She reached down to pet Badem's head, smiling as her purring increased in volume at the touch. "I mean, I just met her...it feels wrong to subject her to surgery. You know what I mean?"

Enes's lips formed a straight line as he nodded. "I understand you. I have people come in here worrying that spaying their dogs or cats is taking away their freedom to make a choice about whether they want to be parents or not."

Celia laughed. "I mean, it's not that. I've heard the yowling sounds of cat sex before and hardly think it sounds like a good time. Or like those cats had a conversation about becoming parents together. Or like the dad is going to stick around and help raise his kittens." She paused then, feeling her cheeks heat. "Did I really just say 'cat sex'? Sorry about that."

"I can handle it. Believe it or not, part of the training to be a veterinarian means not getting squeamish about *any* of the biological processes our little furry friends experience." He pulled a face then. "Plus, I've lived in Istanbul my whole life. It's not like I've never heard cat sex before, either."

"Right." Celia toyed with the handle at the top of the carrier. "So, you think getting Badem spayed is the next right move?"

"Well, it's your decision, of course, not mine. But I do know that the health outcomes look better for female cats who have been spayed. They tend to live longer and be healthier, and as you can imagine, having litters of kittens over and over again can take a real toll on their bodies." He cocked his head to the side, studying her face. "Are you thinking of having Badem inside? Like a full-time inside cat, no more trips out to the garden?"

Celia hesitated then, guilt washing over her. Was he asking because he thought the idea was cruel and unusual? Or because he would miss seeing Badem out in the garden and thought she was being selfish for keeping the cat all to herself? Or was he simply curious about her plans? She decided the only way to find out his intentions was to answer the question.

So she nodded. "I am. I'm still weighing the options, of course. I know she really likes being outside, so I don't want to take that away from her. But...well, it's like you said about spaying. I know cats who live inside tend to be healthier, and of course there are no cars inside, no predators."

Enes nodded back at her. "That's great. Badem will love being an inside cat. Fair warning, she's going to want a lot of attention—"

"Trust me, I figured that out already."

Enes smiled. "Let me guess...she insisted on sleeping in your bed last night? I hope she wasn't bad company."

Celia couldn't quite meet his eyes. Talking about sharing her bed felt intimate...and somehow she couldn't help but switch *him* with Badem in her mind. If she had to guess, based on her imagination alone, *he* wouldn't be bad company at all. "She did," she said, with a brief nod. "How did you know?"

"That's what the previous tenant complained about when he kicked her out."

"Ah." She leaned down close to Badem, kissing her on top of the head. "Well, I didn't mind at all. And I think the two of us will get along just fine."

"I think so, too. Like I was saying, I think she was hanging around outside to be close to the building, the people inside. Not just for food, but for affection and company. Now that she's got that with you, I think she'll be all set."

"I hope you're right."

Enes gave her a toothy grin. "Well, just let me know if you need any help. If this little gal needs more attention than you can give, I'd be happy to come downstairs and give you a bit of a break."

Celia's eyes widened, but she forced herself to nod rather than drop her jaw in shock. "I'm sure we would like that. Wouldn't we, Badem?"

They needed to get out of there before they stopped dancing around it and just started overtly flirting. Nothing about that was a good idea—not the fact that they lived in the same building, that Enes was Badem's vet, or that Celia was still trying to find her footing in Turkey...to say nothing of the fact that she was planning to leave in six months.

She opened the carrier door and scooted Badem inside, faint protestations announcing the cat's displeasure at the enclosure. "So what do I need to do to get her ready for the spaying operation? And when will that happen?"

"Does tomorrow work for you?" When she nodded, he continued speaking. "She shouldn't eat after her dinner tonight. And can you bring her at noon tomorrow?"

Celia checked her watch. "Does this same time work?" She sighed. "Judging by your grimace, it does *not*. It's just that I'm still brand new at the company where I'm consulting, so I can't exactly leave in the middle of the day because of my cat. They don't even expect me to have a cat, a boyfriend, a potted plant, so it's definitely just going to sound like an excuse."

"No boyfriend, good to know." Enes held up his hands to defuse the frown she leveled his way. "Sorry, that came out wrong. I was going to suggest that I could come pick Badem up from your apartment, if that's alright with you. And the fact that there's no boyfriend means there won't be anyone there to be startled by me coming in to your apartment in the middle of the day."

Celia pursed her lips in thought. "You would do that?"

Enes nodded. "Of course. I wouldn't offer that super special service to everyone, but for a customer like you...well, like Badem, really, I'd roll out the red carpet."

"And what, I would just give you my key? I don't have a spare yet..."

"That's fine. You can drop it off with me in the morning and pick it up here at the end of your day. Or actually, why don't you just Bring Badem up to my apartment in the morning? That might be easier for everyone."

"That could work, I guess. What about the procedure? How long would she need to stay at the clinic?"

"I keep them here overnight, and you can pick her up on Saturday morning."

"She'd be here all by herself?" Celia looked around the room, which was somehow sterile and cozy at the same time. "I mean, you don't stay here, of course."

Enes shook his head. "I have cameras to monitor any animals that stay overnight, but in general, after an operation like that, they just sleep all night long. I've never had a cat or a dog do anything else, actually."

Celia was quiet, thoughtful as she looked down at Badem. "Does she have to stay overnight here? I mean, could I bring her home?"

The puzzlement on Enes's face at her first question melted away at the second one. "You could do that if you wanted to. If it made you feel better to have her there." He placed a reassuring hand on her shoulder for just a moment before removing it, back down to the table. "She would be fine here, but if you feel more comfortable being able to keep an eye on her, if you'll rest better...then yes, you can take her home. I could bring her, actually."

Celia waved her hands. "Oh, that's not necessary. I'll come get her and bring her back."

"You're going to carry a cat who's coming out of anesthesia home in a cat carrier?" He raised an eyebrow at her. "Let me drive her. It'll be quicker and you won't be worrying the whole way."

"You drive to work? But it's so close." As the question came out, she didn't know why she'd asked it. What was so wrong with accepting some help from this nice man? And why were his decisions—like whether or not he drove to work—so interesting to her?

"I don't normally, no. But if a special lady like Badem needs a ride home, then I'll be sure to give her one." That hand was back on her shoulder now. "Let me do this, please. I care about Badem, too, and I just want her to be comfortable. Okay?"

Through gritted teeth, Celia said, "Okay," then picked up the carrier, following Enes out to the waiting room.

There, his mom was waiting with the warmest of smiles—so warm that Celia's homesickness threatened to rear its head. This woman had no right to look so sweet, so comforting, so...*motherly* when Celia was on the opposite side of the planet from everyone who cared about her. This was always so much easier when she was surrounded only by colleagues. Then, she could pretend that people outside of the workforce didn't even exist. Children? What were those? Parents? Never heard of them. There were no family members, minimal mixing of generations in the world of consulting, and that's how she got through it.

But as Enes walked over to his mom, placing a large hand on her shoulder and speaking softly to her, Celia felt that twinge again. He wasn't just in the same city as his mom...he was working with her. No, if Celia had understood correctly, he wasn't even working with her. She was just hanging out there because she liked to be near her son and liked to help out when she could.

While mother and son continued to talk to each other, Celia placed the cat carrier on the floor and browsed around the pet supplies lining the walls of the room. If Badem was going to be staying with her long-term, they were going to need to figure out a litter box for her. Toys, too. Celia picked up things as they caught her eye, finally returning to the counter with a new litter box, an assortment of toys and treats, and one of the smaller bags of cat litter.

Enes's mother looked at her son, saying something to him in Turkish that Celia didn't understand. When he nodded, she looked back at Celia and smiled. "My son will drive you home, dear." She gestured to Badem, patiently and silently waiting in her carrier, as well as all the items Celia had collected in her scavenger hunt around the room. "This is too much to carry, and he needs to go home now, anyway. I will close up here."

She opened her mouth to reply, but Enes simply shook his head at her. "Best not to argue with my mother, Celia. She always gets what she wants. And she's right that I do need to go home." He squatted down to put a finger through the bars of Badem's carrier and she moved forward to rub her face against it. "This lady and I have a big day planned tomorrow, so I'd better go home and rest up."

"That's right," his mom chimed in. "You're both tired, aren't you? It's been a long day. I'll bring some food over to you, Enes, and you can share it with this nice woman. What is your name, dear?"

"Celia," she answered. "But that's okay, really. You don't have to—"

"Celia," she interrupted. "That's a pretty name. I'm Meryem. And I won't take no for an answer."

With a laugh and a resigned nod, Celia paid for the examination and the items she was purchasing, then let Enes help her carry it to the door and to a waiting vehicle.

Once Badem and all of her accessories were settled in the backseat, Celia climbed in to the front next to Enes. He slipped the car into gear and began to navigate the streets back to their apartment building.

"So, Celia." He glanced over at her with a smile. "What brings you to Turkey? And, I suppose as your vet, I should ask what makes you ready to take on caregiving for a cat now that you're here?"

She returned a small smile. "Well, I'm here because of my work. I do efficiency consulting for some larger corporations, and I recently accepted a six-month contract in Istanbul."

"I see." He nodded. "That's good work if you can get it. You travel a lot, then?"

"I guess." Celia shrugged. "I mean, I *have* been. For the last few years, it's been a new city, a new contract every six months or so."

"And yet you don't sound excited about that. Why not?" He switched on his turn signal, navigating them down the familiar street that led to their building.

"I don't mean to complain. A lot of people would enjoy the travel, and I certainly have, too."

"But?"

She sighed. "But it does get a bit lonely." She looked back towards the seat behind Enes, where Badem was resting calmly in her carrier. "That's what happened with me and Badem, by the way. I was feeling a bit homesick that day, and then she just wouldn't leave me alone. Wanted to be by my side the whole time. And I don't know what it means, exactly, for my future plans to take a cat on as a sidekick." She shrugged again. "I just couldn't force her out of my life. It felt like...I don't know, like divine intervention maybe?" She scoffed. "I don't know if that even makes sense or if I even believe in such a thing. But I want someone to be with me wherever I go next. And I think Badem will make a great companion."

Enes nodded. "I get it. What about staying in Turkey? Is that on the list of options at all?"

"Maybe. It could be. I do love Istanbul, and Badem wouldn't have to adjust to a new country."

Enes's expression was deadpan. "A very good point. She *does* speak Turkish already and I'm not sure how well she could learn a new language."

Celia felt a small smile playing at the edge of her lips. "If I'm being honest with myself...and why wouldn't I be honest with you, a total stranger?"

"Hey, I must have moved myself up from 'total stranger' status," teased Enes. "Maybe I was a total stranger the other day when you let me into the building. But by now I like to think you could *at least* refer to me as 'Badem's vet.'"

"Fair enough. Can I finish what I was saying, then?"

"Of course." They were in front of the building then, the car parked a short walk away from the garden entrance. Enes switched off the engine, then turned in his seat to watch Celia while she spoke.

"I don't think it's homesickness I was feeling. It's not like I want to move back to St. Louis, and I'm really happy with the frequency with which I get to visit my family. I think I just want to stay in one place long enough to put down roots. Get to know the community. Feel like I'm a part of a neighborhood. Put books on a shelf. And I think that's why I let Badem inside. Why I even stopped to feed her in the first place."

Enes nodded, a smile creeping across his face. "Sounds like you're letting Badem decide for you that you're staying put in Turkey. Not that we—and here I'm speaking on behalf of the entire country—mind. We'd love to keep Badem here within our borders, I mean. Too much brain drain these days...perfectly wonderful and talented cats immigrating to other countries with different opportunities."

"Ah." Celia chuckled. It wasn't *her* he wanted to stay. "I wondered for a second there what you meant, but that makes perfect sense." She gestured toward the door. "Anyway, thanks for the ride. Shall we go inside?"

"Absolutely. I'll help you carry these things upstairs."

And before Celia could protest—she knew he'd ignore it anyway—he had hoisted Badem, her new accessories, and the bag of litter into his arms and was heading towards the door. All she could do was shake her head and jog in front of him to—once again—open the door for Enes.

Seven

The next time Celia saw Enes, it was only about half an hour after he had left her and Badem at her apartment's door. She had appreciated his boundaries, the fact that he hadn't tried to follow her inside—her living room was still a scattered mess considering she had just moved in, and she hadn't washed a dish in the sink since before Badem had come to stay.

But here he was again, and for a moment she had forgotten about the promises his mother had made, finding herself wondering what in the world could bring him back again so soon. Had she forgotten something in his car? Was he coming to check on Badem or to reschedule her appointment for the following morning? Or was it something else…was he coming to pay a social visit, maybe suggest the two of them snuggle up on the couch and kiss a little?

No, it couldn't be that. That wasn't how real life worked, Celia reminded herself. If this were a movie, sure, such a thing was possible. But in reality, neighbors didn't just knock on each other's doors to suggest light making out or to confess to feeling a spark. That would make things too awkward in the building if the feelings weren't reciprocated. Come to think of it, even if both people felt the same way, it could *still* make things awkward in the building. Living in the same building wasn't the same as living together, but it still had the potential to be more intimate than a flirtation or a new relationship had any right to be.

When Celia peeked through the peephole and saw Enes standing there, his gaze was fixed right on the glass of the peephole and his expression was apologetic, as if he knew she'd be eyeballing him out there.

Given that he was a familiar and friendly face, she opened the door, even though no part of her—from her messy bun all the way down to the ragged sweatpants that had traveled the world with her these last few years—was interested in having visitors right now.

"Hi," she greeted him with a smile that she hoped conveyed she didn't *actually* want him to come inside and stay a while. It wasn't that she wouldn't enjoy a visit at *some* point; she just would have preferred at least a *little* warning before that visit began. "What's up? Do you want to come in?" She opened the door only slightly wider, but Enes still shook his head.

"No, that's quite alright," he said with a shake of his head. "I'm sure you're tired, and I am, too. I just wanted to bring this plate from my mom, as promised. It's her specialty, *dolma*." He held up a plate that was heaped with stuffed peppers. "I'm pretty sure you don't want to see or talk to anyone right now, judging by how tired you look, but I couldn't deny my mother." He cocked his head to the side. "I mean, I *could* deny her, but that's a lose-lose-lose situation."

That expression caught Celia's attention. "What's lose-lose-lose about it? I don't think I've heard that expression with three whole 'loses' before." She folded her arms over her chest, waiting for him to explain before she accepted the plate.

Enes shifted his weight. "Well, of course I would lose because I didn't follow my mother's instructions and she would have to tell me all about it tomorrow. Then there's the fact that she would lose—or she would feel like she had lost—because she told you this plate was coming and then it wasn't. Very bad for her reputation. Can't have that. And finally, and perhaps most significantly, you would lose because you wouldn't get to taste *this*."

And with his final word, he lifted the plate close enough for a few smells to waft in Celia's direction. The peppers were still hot, the smell of onions and meat rising with the steam from the rice. Her mouth watered at the interplay of flavors and spices, and she reached out to accept the plate. "Thank you," she said, sincerely. "And thank your mom for me, too, please."

Enes smiled back, giving her a slight nod. "I will. And you'll see her tomorrow, when you come to pick up Badem at the clinic."

"That's right." Celia couldn't help but smile now. It must be something about the plate in her hand and the fact that it felt like comfort food even though she'd never tasted *dolma* before. "I'll bring her up before I leave in the morning. Is that still alright with you?"

"Of course. Have a good night." And before she could thank him or invite him in—was that what she was supposed to do?—the plate was in her hands and he was gone, back up the stairs.

"Hmm." Celia nodded to Badem, who had materialized at her feet once the door was closed. "He's not bad, is he? Is that why you like him so much?" She cocked her head back at Badem, matching the animal's gesture as if the two of them were both trying their hardest to understand each other. "You know, I've never seen an animal that chill with a vet before." She shrugged. "Either *you're* special, or *he* is. Who knows?"

Celia and Badem spent another snuggly night together, both yawning in protest—and one of them meowing as well—when the alarm went off the following morning. Badem continued to meow throughout Celia's morning routine, gentle reminders that it was time for her breakfast. No matter how many times Celia reminded her that she had to fast for her surgery today, the meowing continued. The only time it stopped, actually, was when Celia paused her work preparations to sit on the couch, where Badem promptly curled up next to her, neck extended for chin scratches, her meows replaced with purrs.

"I promise you'll have a delicious tasty meal just as soon as you can eat again. And I'll never make you skip a meal. Deal?" Even though she felt slightly self-conscious about it, Celia packed a snack to eat on her way to work, rather than sitting down for a meal in front of the hungry cat. There was no need to rub it in her face. Besides, she could eat an apple just as easily while walking as she could sitting at the table.

Badem was confused while getting into her carrier, no doubt protesting the hunger strike she had no intentions of taking, but she settled down when the door was closed and they began moving in the direction of Enes's apartment. Just before Celia knocked on the door, she lifted Badem up to peer into the carrier at her. "You really like him, don't you?"

But if Badem was happy to see Enes, it was nothing compared to his reaction at finding the two of them waiting outside his door. His grin was wide, as were his extended arms. And Celia couldn't help but feel that it wasn't just the cat he was greeting, but that he was genuinely that pleased to see her as well. She felt her face warm at the attention, reaching up to ensure her hair was covering her ears rather than broadcasting their redness for the entire building to see.

"Hi, Enes," she greeted him, waving a hand and immediately regretting it. "We're here bright and early, as promised."

"Indeed you are!" He stretched out his arm to take the cat carrier from her, Badem already meowing in greeting. "And how is this lady? Ready for her exciting day today?"

Celia nodded. "She is. No food, no water, no good explanation for why she's hungry and thirsty, but at least she's been a real champ about it." She hesitated, looking down at her feet.

"Something on your mind?"

"Well, it's just..." She bit her lip, looking up to meet his eyes. "This is a standard procedure, right? I mean...it's not high risk or anything, is it? I'm just...I know I'm going to be worrying about her all day, and—"

Enes held up his hand to stop her. "How about I give you a call as soon as the procedure is finished? Would that make you feel better?"

Celia nodded. "It definitely would. Sorry if that's silly or unnecessary, but..." She stopped herself, shaking her head. "You know what? No. I'm not sorry. Badem is a special girl, and it's totally normal to care about your friends when they're having surgery."

Enes nodded back. "I totally agree. And for what it's worth, I do a lot of sterilizations at the clinic. It's one of the more common procedures we do, and I've never once had any complications. Little Miss Badem is going to be just fine."

"Thank you. You're still going to call me, right? Even though you've reassured me that this is no big deal?"

"Of course. Let me just grab my phone and get your number." He ducked back inside, taking Badem with him. Celia said a silent farewell to her feline friend in her head, wishing for the first time since she started her contractor career that she could take a personal day.

When Enes returned—without Badem, who Celia could hear meowing faintly from another room—the two of them exchanged phone numbers, along with a few more reassurances that everything was going to be okay and that they would be speaking about the cat's status soon.

As Celia tucked her phone back into her purse and prepared to depart, she jolted, hitting her palm against her forehead. "Oh shoot! I totally forgot about your mom's plate. I was going to bring it to give it back to you. Do you want me to run downstairs and grab it now?"

"Not necessary at all." A mischievous grin crossed his face. "Actually, you know we never return an empty plate in Turkey?"

"What do you mean? You don't want me to keep the plate, do you?"

He shook his head. "No, it's still a good idea to return it. No need for you to start collecting plates. Plus, now that my mom knows you live in my building, I'm sure she'll want to send over food more often. If you keep the plate every time, she won't have any dishes left."

"Okay...then what exactly do you want me to do? Please explain this to me like I know nothing about Turkish culture, because that would not be completely inaccurate."

Enes grinned. "Alright, fine. I'll put you out of your misery. Just put something on the plate when you return it. You don't have to cook something yourself, but even a piece of fruit or something. It's a nice gesture, and when I pass it along to my mother, she'll be very happy about it." He shrugged then. "Of course, if you are too busy to put something on the plate, I'll just tell her you hated her *dolma*. That might keep it from coming in the future." In response to the horrified expression on Celia's face, he put up a hand in protest. "I'm kidding. I wouldn't say that to my mother, and I wouldn't throw my new neighbor under the bus like that. I'd probably just put something from my own fridge on the plate when I gave it back to her."

Celia shook her head. "You don't have to do that. I'll think of something and give it to you soon. Tomorrow?"

"Any time is fine." He glanced at his watch. "I think you need to leave for work soon, yes? And Miss Badem and I are going to need to head out soon, too."

"Okay, yes. Good luck today. Not that you need it. Just...let me know, okay? How everything goes?"

Enes nodded, placing one reassuring hand on her forearm. "I will, I promise. Badem will be fine. Better than fine. Once she comes out of anesthesia and her scar heals, she'll be healthier and happier than she would have been, living outside and having litter after litter of kittens."

"Okay." Celia nodded a few times, steeling herself for the day ahead. "If you say so. Thank you, Enes." She placed her other hand on top of his, just for a second, before turning to leave.

Eight

The day couldn't go by quickly enough for Celia's comfort. Enes had texted her around noon to let her know they would be beginning the procedure soon, and he had called her a surprisingly short time later to report that everything had gone swimmingly and that Badem would be waking up from the anesthesia just in time for Celia to come pick her up.

She had nearly cried with relief at his voice. How, after all these years of non-attachment and refusing to put down roots, was she now this attached to Badem, and this quickly after meeting her? It was frightening. Inconvenient. It didn't align with her lifestyle at all.

"Is everything okay?" Ayla asked from across the table after Celia had hung up with Enes. She gestured towards Celia's face. "You looked so worried."

Celia shook her head. "Everything's fine. My cat got spayed today, and that was her vet, just calling to say the procedure went well."

Ayla's forehead crinkled with a frown. "You have a cat? I thought you just moved here. Did you bring it with you?"

"No, I just met her a few days ago. It's all happened so fast." Celia laughed, but it was forced. "I haven't really thought it all through yet."

Ayla was quiet, thoughtful. "Well, if you need a place for her to stay when your contract ends, my parents feed a lot of cats in their neighborhood. I'm sure she would fit right in."

It was a kind offer, Celia knew that. So why was it making her feel so angry? So possessive? She barely stopped herself from leaping across the table and grabbing Ayla's collar, scolding her for wanting to take her cat away from her. Instead, she forced a smile and nodded. "Thanks for the offer. I'll figure something out. I don't think I could let her go even if I wanted to."

"Maybe you'll stay in Istanbul then." Ayla's eyes lit up with excitement. "Apply for a residence permit—my cousin's girlfriend did that, and it wasn't too complicated—and make it your home. You would love it here. I mean, I know you're already here. But it's different when you live here. When you're not just visiting."

"Maybe." Celia took a bite of her chickpeas and rice, the effort to chew feeling monumental. "But it's too soon to make any long-term plans. Maybe Badem and I—that's what I named the cat, Badem—will travel together."

Ayla pulled a face, her eyes opening their widest yet. "Have you ever been on an airplane with a cat? I keep seeing videos on Instagram of cats who love to travel, but I don't think I've met one in real life yet."

Celia fell silent then, no longer forcing herself to respond, as the worries and concerns of her new life as a pet owner threatened to overtake her mind. What was she doing? Had she thought any of this through? Was it even possible for her to commit to an animal when her lifestyle was so diametrically opposed to it?

Too many questions. And none of them were going to get answered today. She excused herself from the table and made her way back to her desk, the distraction of work more welcome than ever.

Nine

Celia made it to the vet's office as quickly as she could, making one speedy stop at a small market to pick up a few ingredients she needed for her evening plans.

She was greeted at the door by Enes's mother, her smile even wider and her presence even more welcoming than it had been the last time they had met.

"Welcome back, Celia!" She pulled her in for an embrace and a double cheek kiss. "Your little Badiş is such a sweet girl, and I just know she will be so happy to see you."

"Thank you, Meryem," said Celia, an influx of emotion bubbling up in her throat, both with relief and at the nickname Meryem had bestowed on Badem. "And thank you so much for the *dolma*. It was really delicious."

"Oh, don't mention it, *canım*. You're very welcome."

"Did you hear that, Badiş? Your mom is here!" Enes's deep voice echoed down the hallway, along with the sound of his footsteps. He appeared in front of Celia just a moment later, with a toothy grin and a very sleepy Badem crouching in her cat carrier.

"Hi, you!" Celia bent down, poking a finger in the cage. "Is she okay? She looks kind of out of it."

Enes nodded. "She just came out of the anesthesia, so it's going to be a while before she's back to her bouncy self. She will be like this for most of the evening, but it's perfectly normal. If she were staying here for the night, she'd just be in her cage snoozing away. As long as you don't expect any playfulness from her tonight—or any appetite, either—then anything else is normal."

"Okay, thank you." Celia took the carrier from him, not quite able to meet his eyes. Her confusion about the future for her and for Badem was suddenly making her feel very shy and not a little silly. He was probably judging her for subjecting the poor creature to surgery when she didn't even know where the two of them would be in half a year. What kind of person did that?

But that was a question for another day. After a brief conversation with his mother, Enes was once again leading her towards his car to take the two of them home—the *three* of them, Celia reminded herself. He was only doing this for Badem.

Conversation was stilted in the car. Celia could blame it on the fact that she was sitting in the back seat this time, devoting the vast majority of her attention to the woozy cat next to her. But, if she let her mind go there, she could also blame it on the fact that Enes was just doing a kindness for someone he didn't know and, frankly, wasn't that interested in knowing. Once he returned her to her apartment, that would be it for the two of them, unless she needed to take Badem to his office again in the future.

They said their goodbyes at the entrance to her apartment, and Celia thanked him for all he had done, for her and for Badem. Once she was inside, with the cat carrier in one hand and the bag of groceries in the other, she remembered the ambitious plans she had made earlier in the evening, before she had realized quite how groggy Badem was going to be. She had bought ingredients to make brownies, planning to return the plate to Enes with a heaping pile of them on it.

"Right." She was talking to herself again, carrying the groceries into the kitchen before taking Badem to the bed to get comfortable. "Let's get you settled in here, ma'am, and then I'll get to work in the kitchen."

Badem was wobbly as she came out of the carrier, but with a little help from Celia, she settled down on one of the pillows and seemed to fall immediately asleep. Celia stayed to pet her, unnerved by the lack of purrs that usually issued so freely from Badem, and once she was sure her animal companion was soundly sleeping, she returned to the kitchen and got to work.

She was mixing the dry ingredients in a bowl when she heard a thud from the bedroom. Heart racing, she ran in to find Badem on the floor, not the bed where she had left her, doing a good impression of a zombie as she lurched towards the kitchen.

"Sweet girl, no! What are you doing? No jumping, okay? You're going to hurt yourself. Just stay there, okay?" But Badem was still taking her jolting steps towards the open kitchen and living room, clearly uninterested in being left alone in her time of recovery.

The problem repeated itself in the living room. Celia thought she had Badem settled on the couch there, but once again, she jumped off, wanting to come closer than she already was. Celia was nearly in tears—and the brownies were nearly in the oven—as she gently escorted Badem back into the carrier.

"I'm sorry, honey," she said. "I just don't know what to do to keep you safe." As an idea occurred, she got to her feet and began walking toward the door. "Wait there, okay? I'll be right back."

Before she knew what she was doing, her hand was poised in the air after knocking on Enes's door, and the door was opening before she had time to drop it back down to her side.

"What's wrong?" he asked, his eyes full of concern as he pulled the door open. "Is everything okay?"

"Yes, but..." Celia bit her lip. "Badem is just a little ambitious right now, and she keeps jumping off of furniture instead of staying put and sleeping off her medicine. I don't want to overreact, but—"

"No, it's good you came up here. She could rip her stitches or hurt herself." He reached back, grabbing a cardigan. "Where is she now? Do you want me to come down and take a look?"

Celia nodded, overcome with relief. "She's in her carrier again, and I think she's fine. I didn't want to poke around at her stitches or anything and risk making it worse. I was just..."

The two of them were making their way down the stairs now. "I was trying to make some brownies for when I return the plate to you, and I couldn't do two things at once, and Badem clearly wanted to be close to me and I couldn't figure out—"

"You're making me brownies?" Enes flashed her a wide grin as she opened the door. "I'm glad you came to me for help, then. Anything I can do to help that treat become a reality, I will absolutely do. I love brownies."

Celia felt herself blush. "That's good to know. And yeah, I wanted to make them for you because I don't want to return an empty plate and also because you deserve to have nice things done for you. You've been really helpful to the two of us, and I don't know a better way to express that than with chocolate and homemade baked goods."

"I have to agree," he said. "They do say the way to a man's heart is through his stomach, though I don't think that's necessarily gender specific. After all, I get the impression you love my mother now that you've tasted her cooking."

"Oh absolutely." Celia nodded fervently. They were in the living room now, and she was opening the door to Badem's carrier, both of them crouching down in front of the small container. "If your mom wanted to make me an honorary member of the family, I'd accept in a heartbeat."

"That's good to know." It was Enes's turn to have red cheeks, Celia noticed, as he adjusted his position to take a seat. She was probably making him uncomfortable with all of her overt affection. Better to focus their attention back to the reason he had come—Badem.

Enes was examining Badem now, who had climbed onto his outstretched legs and was slowly making her way up his lap.

"She looks fine," he said, gently touching her belly as she settled down on his legs. "I think she just wants to be near someone for comfort or maybe for warmth." He leaned back against the couch. "If you want, I can sit here with her while you finish making the brownies."

"Really?" Celia shook her head. "You must be tired after a long day of work, and the last thing you want to do is spend more time doing the same thing you've been doing all day. No, it's okay. Now that I know everything is fine, I'll just keep her in the carrier until I can give her my full attention. Really."

But Enes just smiled and shook his head in response. "I wouldn't have offered if I minded, Celia. I care about Badem and about you, and I don't want you worrying about her. Especially not when there are brownies in the equation." His expression sobered. "No, but seriously. I'll be doing the same thing here that I would have been doing up in my apartment—just hanging out, really." He rubbed his chin. "Uh...but, well, at least here there is company. It was feeling a little lonely up there after I said goodbye to the two of you, so you'd be doing me a favor, too."

"Are you sure?"

"Absolutely." He gestured for her to get back to the countertop, where her brownie batter was waiting. "Do what you were doing. Badiş is okay, and I'm just here hanging out with my two friends." He dug his phone out of his pocket, doing his best not to jostle Badem in the process. "I was just about to order some dinner when you knocked, so what sounds good to you?" He shot her a look. "And before you can say, 'no, that's not necessary,' just trust me that this is going to happen. It's an even trade, really. Brownies for kebap. Trust me."

Celia shook her head, a chuckle escaping as she got back to stirring the brownie batter one last time. "Just order two of whatever you were going to get. I don't know that much about Turkish food yet, so I'm not picky. I just want to try it all."

"Challenge accepted," said Enes as his fingers sailed over the phone screen. His attention was intense, not a word spoken between them as he tapped away on his phone and she slid the tray into the oven.

It felt oddly homey, having him there, not strange at all like she would have feared. There were comfortable silences, but there was conversation, too. At one point, he picked up Badem carefully in his arms, relocating the two of them to a more comfortable position on the couch, and Celia's heart skipped at the sight of the handsome man with the small, sleeping cat cradled in his arms. After she finished cleaning up, she joined him on the couch, reaching for the remote on the coffee table.

"Do you want to watch a movie or something?" she asked, gesturing to the television on the wall.

"Whatever you want," he said. "I'm all yours."

Celia's cheeks flushed at his choice of words, and she set about finding something fun and distracting—and not at all romantic—to watch together. Ten minutes later, she was still searching when a knock sounded on the door.

"That will be the food." Enes got to his feet, kissing Badem on the top of the head before depositing her gently on Celia's lap.

As his arm brushed against hers, right before he left to meet the delivery person at the door, she shook herself. He wasn't hers, just because he was here. He wasn't her boyfriend—or even her friend—just because it might look that way to an outside observer at this moment.

They were just a vet and a patient enjoying some takeout food and watching a movie together on the couch.

But even as she thought that, she laughed out loud at it. No, there was nothing normal about what was happening right now. She looked down at Badem's sleeping face and leaned closer. "Do you know what's happening, Badem?"

She thought—but possibly imagined—that she heard a small murmur, the first since they had returned to the apartment. That had to be a good sign. She tried again. "Was this your doing? Are you trying to make something happen here, lady?"

That time, the chirp originating from Badem was unmistakable, and the sound popped out just as Enes came back into the room.

"Well, it sounds like someone woke up!" His grin was broad. "How's our girl doing? What are you two talking about?"

You, Celia wanted to say. *What you're doing here. How easily you group the two of us together and make her "our" girl. The fact that Badem might have some grand master plan to set the two of us up with each other. Too bad she doesn't have a better grasp on geography and the nature of short-term international contract work.*

Instead, she just smiled. "I think she's feeling a little better." She widened her eyes at the bag in his hand. "And

I'm feeling a little hungry and can't wait to see what's in that bag."

It turned out that what was in that bag was, in fact, a feast. At the revelation that Celia hadn't tried a lot of Turkish food, Enes had apparently worked his way through the menu available at one of his favorite restaurants, choosing a selection of grilled meats and meatballs, vegetables, bulgur, salad...he just kept opening containers, and her eyes got wider with every one.

They arranged the dishes on the coffee table, Badem sleeping on the couch between them as they piled their plates high and finally started to watch something. Celia hadn't been able to find a movie, but once Enes mentioned he'd never seen *The Office*, they started streaming that from the beginning.

Episode after episode passed. The takeout containers—nearly empty—were cleared away, replaced by a tray of brownies that the two of them dug into with the enthusiasm of two people who *hadn't* just eaten a massive dinner.

Celia leaned forward to scoop the corner piece out of the pan, frowning. "So much for sending you home with a plate piled high with these. There goes my whole plan."

Enes placed a reassuring hand on her elbow. "Trust me, it's far better this way. I've had more fun here with you and Badem than I would have upstairs alone by far." He leaned back, a sigh escaping his lips. "In fact, I could get used to this. What do you say we make these hangouts a regular thing, at least until we finish watching *The Office*?"

Celia's eyes goggled at him. "Really? You want to hang out with me that much? There are a *lot* of episodes."

Enes's eyes were locked on hers as he nodded. "Absolutely. I've missed having someone to come home to, but if we can at least enjoy our time, share some meals, and laugh at a silly show together, won't that help both of us feel a little less alone here?"

She shook her head. "You're *not* alone here, though. Your mom, at least, lives here, and probably the rest of your family, too, right? You must have friends, maybe even a girlfriend." She shrugged. "And I'm just here, the foolish person who moved to the opposite side of the ocean from her entire family and now is surprised that she gets lonely sometimes. Apart from Badem, I don't have anyone here. I mean, I have some friendly colleagues, but that's not the same."

He swallowed. "You have me. I'm right upstairs."

"No." She bit her lip, surprised by her own honesty but unable to stop it. "It's not the same. Because you're up there, I know I'm not alone in the building, sure." She gestured around her. "But there's no one here, nothing making this place feel like home."

"And do you want that?"

Celia gave a hesitant nod. "Maybe. It doesn't really fit with the nature of my work, but I don't know if I can keep doing this forever." She reached to the cushion between them, where Badem was sleeping, rubbing the back of her neck. "I think this little girl made me realize that, actually. I think that's why she chose me. To tell me it's going to be time to slow down a little soon." She shrugged. "Maybe put down some roots. Stay somewhere for longer than I normally do."

"Love someone." At the startled look on her face, he put up his hands. "Badem, I mean. Though you could probably try loving something a little bigger at some point, too. A dog or a horse...maybe even a human."

"I will definitely think about giving that a try." Celia nodded, leaning forward to pick up the remote. "What do you think, another episode? I don't want to keep you if you need to get back."

Enes checked his watch. "Oh, it's still early. Let's do this."

Ten

Celia woke the next morning with such a crick in her neck that she was temporarily convinced she had lost all ability to move it. She groaned as she rubbed the knot forming just above her shoulder. As her vision came into focus, confusion eclipsed the pain she was feeling.

"What in the—? Why am I on the couch?" She lifted her feet off the coffee table, placing them on the ground as she looked down to see the source of the weight on her lap, jumping to her feet in shock when she realized what the cause was.

Because there, on her lap, had been Enes's sock-clad feet. At the realization that their TV marathon had turned into a sleepover on the couch, Celia began looking around frantically for Badem, guilt consuming her.

They had done all of this for her. To keep her comfortable and help her get the rest she needed to heal. And yet Celia had been so distracted by a cute neighbor that she had fallen asleep practically cuddling with him—okay, it was just his feet on her lap, but still—and now she had no idea where Badem was.

She wasn't in the bedroom. Not in the litter box. Not in the cat bed or the cozy chair in the living room.

Of course, there was one place Celia didn't want to look, but that was only because she was too concerned about the reaction she would have if she looked in Enes's direction. He was still sleeping, after all, and it was too intimate, wasn't it? It was one thing when they were both unconscious, but if only he was sleeping, and if she looked at him...well, that was too much like something people in love with each other would do. And what if he woke up and caught her looking at him? How embarrassed would she be then?

As Celia was searching the furthest—and least likely to hold a cat—corners of the living room, she heard a faint Badem chirp from the couch, and she couldn't avoid it any more.

And sure enough, the sight she had been hoping to see—Badem, looking rested and more like herself—was right there in the same image as the sight she'd been avoiding. Because sure enough, Enes was snuggled up on her couch like he belonged there with a cat nestled on his chest.

So relieved was she to see Badem out of the influence of the anesthesia that Celia rushed over, petting her, talking to her quietly, and even bending down to kiss her on the head—*the same place Enes had kissed the cat yesterday*, an annoying part of her brain reminded her. Naturally, it was at that moment that Enes awoke, blinking rapidly, no doubt at the sight of Celia crouched over him, murmuring and making kissy sounds.

"Good morning," he said, his voice even deeper in the morning and his eyes adorably sleepy.

"Yikes, sorry. Hi." Celia leaped back. "Didn't mean to startle you." She cleared her throat. "And, er...good morning. I don't know how we fell asleep here, but I'm sorry you didn't get to sleep in a comfy bed last night."

Enes shook his head. "Not at all. I was aware of the decision I was making."

"What do you mean?"

"Well, you drifted off to sleep there, and then Badem was asleep on my lap." He shrugged. "I didn't want to wake either one of you up, so I just switched off the show and closed my eyes. And here we are."

"Huh." Celia was flabbergasted. "Yeah, here we are, I guess. Did you get some rest at least?"

"I think so." He patted Badem, who sat up a little straighter under his touch. "This little gal is a great cuddle buddy."

Celia nodded. "She definitely is. That's one of the first things I really loved about her. And she's looking great this morning, almost back to herself."

"She is. I don't think she'll be hungry quite yet, but maybe you can offer her some food and water later in the day. She's going to be sleeping a lot still, but that's good. That's where the healing happens."

"Thank you." Celia placed her hand on the least sensual part of Enes she could find—and it was a challenge, considering how appealing he was looking to her—his shin. "For everything. And especially for staying over here. It really eased my mind. I think I'll stick around the house today to keep an eye on her. So if you have Saturday plans and need to get going, well, then by all means, don't let us keep you."

"That's right, it's Saturday." He yawned and stretched. "No plans, actually." He glanced at the coffee table, the television, and finally back at Celia. "But if you're going to be stuck inside today, would you be up for a second round? I could go pick up some breakfast pastries and we could resume the marathon. Do you have a way to make coffee?"

"I do, but..." Celia stopped herself from once again telling Enes that he didn't have to be here. He was a free man, and she could try believing that he meant what he said, that he wasn't offering merely out of obligation. "That would be great. I would love to spend some more time with you, and I'm sure Badem would, too. I've got coffee and milk. Is that good or do you need anything else? Sugar?"

"I'm fine, honey." He chuckled. "I always wanted to make that joke, and it's just as cheesy as I thought it would be." He eyed the empty pan on the table. "I wish there were some more brownies to go along with that coffee, but I'll see if I can find some kind of weak substitute for them at the bakery." He sat up, easing Badem off his lap and back onto the couch. "I should head out then. I'll be quick."

"Okay." She smiled at him as he left the room, second guessing the question she so desperately wanted to ask. What *was* this between the two of them? Should she ask? Risk making things awkward between them by finding out that they had conflicting intentions? As she heard the door close behind Enes, she shook her head. Six months was a far cry from forever, but it would *feel* like an eternity if things were tense and weird between her and the only neighbor she knew. Better just to enjoy his company and let it be.

A purr escaped from Badem for the first time since the procedure, and Celia grinned at the sound she hadn't realized she'd been craving. "Oh, so you approve of the plan, then?" she asked, scratching the cat under her chin. "You like having Enes around? Of course you do."

Me too, she thought to herself. *Maybe a little too much.*

Eleven

The three of them fell into a comfortable routine, so easily and naturally that Celia kept waiting for the rug to be pulled out from underneath her. But every evening, like clockwork, Enes turned up at her door shortly after she got home, bearing a home-cooked meal courtesy of Meryem at least a couple of times each week, and the two of them—with Badem in between—settled in to enjoy dinner, conversation, and a few more episodes of *The Office*.

"Thank goodness there are so many episodes of that show," she said to Badem one night after closing the door behind Enes. "When it's over, what are we going to do?" She frowned as a thought occurred to her. Certainly, she and Enes could find something else to watch together...but was that even what he wanted? It was the show that had hooked him, after all, not the pleasure of her company. And what else could compare to *The Office*?

It was a concern she could postpone for a while, anyway, considering that they were only on the third season. By the time the credits rolled in the last episode, they might be sick of spending time together.

There was no indication that time was coming soon, though. Every time there was a knock on Celia's door, her heart rate picked up and she found a grin spreading across her face. *How nice to be Enes,* she thought, as she tried to suppress her broad smile, play things just a bit cooler, *greeted with nothing short of sheer joy every time the door opens.*

It wasn't just Celia who was happy to see him, either. Badem had taken to greeting Enes with loud, insistent chirps, which only stopped when he picked her up, kissed her repeatedly on the top of the head, and asked her about her day. Even after that, she rarely left his side when they were all on the couch together, choosing his lap over Celia's ninety percent of the time.

"I'm not offended," Celia told Enes, while shaking her head at the cat currently making biscuits just above his knee. "I know she loves me."

"Of course she does," Enes agreed. "How could she not? She's just giving you a break, I think. Spreading the love."

Celia nodded. She needed to be careful. It was too easy to feel like the three of them were a little family, like Enes was spending time with her because there was *something* between them and not simply because he enjoyed comedy and preferred not to spend his evenings alone. If she didn't give herself regular reminders of the facts, she was liable to end up heartbroken when he started dating someone and suddenly became less available.

Not that it mattered. Whether Enes was about to lose himself in a relationship or not, the clock was ticking on their time together. And if her heart was getting this wrapped up in her neighbor, then the escape of the next contract couldn't come soon enough. But why did her stomach clench when she trotted out that thought to ground herself?

Twelve

In the interest of not getting too attached to Badem's vet—though it was already too late for that, if she was being honest—Celia began to spend the occasional evening out in the city with Ayla. The younger woman had been only too eager to help Celia get better acquainted with Istanbul, and even though nothing beat being at home—*at my apartment,* she reminded herself, *not my home*—she was thoroughly enjoying the sights and experiences Istanbul had to offer.

The two of them had spent time in Sultanahmet, Celia awed into silence at the old buildings, the beautiful architecture, the history. They had visited entirely too many cute cafes to keep track of, gone shopping in Taksim, and on that particular evening they were on a ferry cruising across the Bosphorus.

Celia took a deep breath, closing her eyes to focus her attention on the wind in her hair, the taste of salt in the breeze. "I really love it here," she told Ayla as she met her gaze. "There's just something about this city." Another deep breath. "I could live here for a lifetime and never get tired of it."

Ayla smiled back, but there was a hint of sadness in her eyes. "It's too bad you're leaving then." She leaned against the railing, looking out at the water spreading to both sides of the ship. "Does it make you sad? All the change? All the places and people you've left behind?"

Though her first instinct was to shake her head and reassure Ayla that she loved her jet-set lifestyle, to focus on the positive until she saw a hint of jealousy in her companion, she opted for honesty and nodded. "It does. Not always." The sun was rapidly approaching the horizon, shades of orange streaking through the darkening blue. "This one will make me sad." She exhaled a humorless laugh. "That's the first time I've admitted that out loud. And I know it's time to start thinking about the next contract, to line something up for when my work finishes here." She shrugged. "It's just so hard to make myself do it, though. And I don't know why."

"Really?" Ayla's expression was incredulous as she shook her head. "Come on, it can't be a mystery."

Celia recoiled slightly at her friend's tone. "No, I really don't know why. I've done this plenty of times before, but something is different here and it's really bugging me. The sooner I figure out a new plan, the better it will be."

Ayla shook her head. "Why does it always have to be that, though? Why can't you stay? It sounds like that's what you want, Celia." She turned her head back to the horizon. "You love it here. You adopted a cat. You have a crush on that neighbor of yours, no matter how much you don't want to admit it. And it's okay to make a different choice. Or to realize that all the choices you've made thus far have led you right to where you are and then to just...well, to just stop making new choices. To stay. To enjoy it."

Celia was quiet, grateful for the lack of eye contact. Ayla had seen right into her soul, it seemed, and if she looked into Celia's eyes right now, she would see the truth there. That everything she had said was just exactly what Celia wanted. That the last thing she wanted to do now was to pack her suitcase, say goodbye to Enes, and get on an airplane with Badem.

"How would that even work?" She asked the question so softly she was surprised when Ayla turned to her in response, eyes wide. "I mean, people don't get to just decide to live in a new city, in a different country. There are things like passports and visas and all that." She shook her head. "It's too big a commitment. And it will probably scare Enes away, can you imagine? Sure, he might enjoy hanging out with me now, but when I tell him I'm never leaving?" She huffed out a single laugh. "Just wait and see how quickly that man runs for the hills."

Ayla was silent, but the look she gave Celia spoke volumes. She wasn't buying it, the excuses Celia was giving her. But, thankfully, it seemed like she wasn't going to push the matter any further tonight, and Celia could at least appreciate that.

Thirteen

Alone—except, of course, for Badem—in her room that night, Celia was wide awake, staring up in the direction of the ceiling. The room was too dark to see anything, the perfect canvas for the familiar thoughts, worries, fears...and a few new possibilities that were swirling through her mind. "What if I stayed?" she murmured, saying the words out loud for her ears only. Badem heard them too, though, a soft sound of her own pushed out in response, but she didn't move. At least one of them was sleeping.

But what Celia was doing was better than sleep. She nestled deeper into her pillows and felt a smile spread across her face as her imagination ran away with this new possibility. What if she lived here? What if she put her suitcase away in a closet for so long that she forgot where it was? What if she bought a bookshelf and started filling it up with paperbacks, something that had always seemed too impractical, too incompatible with her lifestyle? What if she settled in, let herself feel at home somewhere rather than just seeing it as another stop on her ongoing journey?

If that journey was going to bring her somewhere, eventually…then why not Istanbul? The city certainly had plenty to offer. And if it was good enough for 15 million people, then why not her?

It was almost impossible to fall asleep that night, as her imagination kept taking hold of new potential realities that might come into being if Celia Long packed up her passport holder and stayed put.

One potential that kept revisiting her was Enes. What, if anything, would happen between them when she told him she was staying? *If* she told him she was staying, she reminded herself. Just because it sounded like fun didn't mean it was going to happen. There was a very real possibility that in the light of day, none of this would seem like a good idea. And there were still all the logistics to think about…

Yeah, yeah. But what if? Would he sweep her up in his arms and kiss her for the first time? Well, that was a nice possibility to imagine. But what if that wasn't his response? What if he smiled politely and wished her well, setting boundaries that hadn't seemed necessary when the clock was ticking on her time remaining in his city?

One thing at a time, Celia reminded herself. *Tomorrow, I'll start at square one. The job.*

Fourteen

Celia hadn't spent much time in the office of the CEO of Aslanbey Holding. It wasn't that Kemal Aslanbey wasn't friendly, hadn't extended the invitation. But Celia had plenty to do already, more than enough ways to spend her time as she unraveled the knot that was Aslanbey Holding's convoluted processes, and sipping a cup of tea with the boss had seemed, frankly, like a waste of time.

That thought might come back to bite me in the ass, Celia thought, as she pasted on a smile, took a sip of her tea, and waited for Kemal to respond. She had just, as casually as possible, asked if there was any possibility of staying on at Aslanbey Holding in a more permanent capacity, and his inscrutable expression was giving nothing away.

Kemal deposited a sugar cube in his tea glass, the small spoon clanging against the side like a delicate bell as he stirred it. He took a sip and exhaled from the heat of the liquid as he set the cup back down on the saucer on the table in front of him. His smile was apologetic as he shook his head. "I'm afraid not, Celia. You've done great work, of course, and I know you will continue to do so over the remainder of your contract." He met her eyes, his lips pulling in at the corners. "But I'm afraid you've been so efficient that, well, you've worked yourself right out of the job. What would an efficiency consultant even do in a full-time capacity?"

"Oh, it doesn't have to be...I mean, I wouldn't expect to be working in the same capacity. I just...I'd do something different. I just want to be here."

"Here in Istanbul? Or here at Aslanbey Holding?"

"...both?"

Kemal's smile was more genuine then. "You wouldn't be the first person who was just passing through Istanbul who fell in love with the city and decided to stay. But I'm afraid I can't help you with that. Even if we could find work for you, there's the reality of visas and all the paperwork that goes along with that. We aren't equipped to deal with that. I hope you understand."

Celia nodded once. "I do." She shifted forward in her chair, about to get to her feet. "And thank you for your time, sir. I really appreciate it."

Kemal studied her face. "You'll figure it out, Celia, if you want it badly enough. And if you do stay, then don't be a stranger. You're welcome for tea anytime." He gestured towards the cup in front of her, the same one she had been about to abandon in her rush to bolt out of his office.

Celia forced a smile and took a few more sips before making an excuse about another meeting she had to get to and leaving Kemal's office. But there were no more meetings scheduled today, other than the meeting between her head and her desk as she slumped in her chair, brought her forehead to the smooth, cool surface, and groaned.

It wasn't going to happen. This wasn't going to work. If Kemal, the one person she knew in this city who had any hiring power, didn't want to invest the time and effort in hiring her, then who else would? It had been a pipe dream, and she knew it...but now even that dream had slipped through her fingers.

And Celia knew what that meant. Tonight, when she was back in her apartment, it was time to start looking for her next contract.

Fifteen

Celia had canceled her regular evening plans with Enes. She needed to focus on figuring out her next move, and she wasn't ready to talk about it with him yet. She was sitting on the couch, laptop perched on her lap and Badem snoozing beside her, one reassuring paw placed on the side of Celia's thigh.

There were a few different leads to choose from, thanks to her networking skills and the various online systems that she had put in place to capture them. The only problem was that none of them were exciting to her. Since she had allowed herself to imagine a future in Istanbul, nothing else could compare. Everything felt like a loss—moving was a tragedy now, not an adventure.

"That's a tiny bit dramatic, isn't it?" she said out loud as she took a sip of wine. "There's got to be something good in here."

But the butterflies that she normally relied on, the fluttering excitement that always told her "this is it, this is the one" were missing. And they didn't come back, no matter how much she chastised herself for their absence.

But if she couldn't use emotion to make this choice, then she could use ration. Logic. That beautiful brain of hers that companies were vying to rent on contract. And through that lens, she could see that taking a contract in Germany made the most sense. There were two different options, one in Berlin and one in Frankfurt. The pay was good, and it would be a relatively short journey for Badem.

"Badem," Celia said, reaching over to stroke the sleeping cat's ear. Was it cruel to subject the cat to an international move? Would she enjoy the adventure, just happy to be near Celia? Or would she be happier here, in the city, the garden that she knew, even if Celia wasn't there any longer? Celia, for one, knew that she didn't want to be parted from the animal. But she couldn't help but feel a pang of guilt at the thought of putting her in a cage and taking her on an airplane, where no amount of explanation could help her understand why her ears were hurting, why she couldn't come out of the cage, why everything was so loud, so bumpy.

But the thought of leaving her behind was unbearable, too. What, was she supposed to just take Badem back out to the building's garden and leave her there? Tears started to slide down her face at the mere thought of walking away while the uncomprehending cat meowed behind her. She could never do that.

Maybe she could ask Enes to take her. *Not forever*, she reassured herself. *Just for a couple of days while I go to Germany and scope things out.*

And with that thought, she found her feet carrying her to the door and up the stairs to his apartment, where she knocked and waited. She wiped her eyes, aware for a brief moment that since the emotions had started bubbling up on the couch, she hadn't so much as glanced in a mirror. *Oh well.*

"Celia?" Enes opened the door, a smile immediately replaced by a frown as his eyes searched her face. "Is everything okay?"

She nodded, then shook her head as the tears began to flow anew. "Not really. No."

"Is it Badem? Do you need me?"

"She's fine. But I do need your help, I think. I...well, you know I can't stay in Istanbul forever, right?"

Enes looked concerned, confused. "I know you're here on a contract, yeah. Why?"

"I need to line up my next contract, and I think I need to spend a few days in Germany to do that."

"...okay?"

"And I was wondering if you could watch Badem."

"Oh." Relief crossed Enes's face. "Of course. I thought there was something wrong, Celia." A hint of a smile. "You shouldn't worry me like that."

"What were you worried about?"

Enes shrugged. "I thought you were leaving already. But you're coming back, right? This isn't one of those Irish goodbyes I've heard about, is it?"

That got a small chuckle out of Celia. "It's not. I wouldn't leave you with my cat and just...disappear."

"I know." He placed a hesitant yet reassuring hand on her forearm. "But you could leave her with me, you know. If you needed to, I mean. I know it's not easy to travel with animals, and I want you to know that. I know it would be very sad for you to even think about that, and I don't want to make you feel bad. So just know that it's an option, okay?"

Celia couldn't speak, so she just nodded. He was kinder and better than she had even known, and she'd already been impressed by Enes's heart, his selfless nature. But it was as if he had seen the concern in her eyes and wanted to ease it before she had even expressed it to him, before she had even fully expressed it to herself. It made it even worse to think about leaving him. And if she left him and Badem together? Well, the two of them clearly deserved each other, as special as they were. And they would be happy together, too, of that she was sure. But if she would be sad without Badem, she would be *miserable* without the two of them. "Thank you," she managed, lifting a hand in a feeble wave as she turned to make her way back down the stairs.

But she didn't make it far. Enes's hand, still on her forearm, encircled her wrist and pulled gently as he took a step forward, taking her into his arms, holding her against his chest. Celia took a sharp intake of surprised breath and then let herself relax into the embrace, let her arms come around his back.

"Sorry," he mumbled in her ear. "You looked like you needed a hug, but I should have asked."

She shook her head, her cheek rubbing against his chest. "I did," she said. "And if you had asked, I probably would have just cried harder."

He pulled back but didn't release her, his eyes finding hers. "Is everything okay, Celia? If…if leaving makes you feel this sad, then…well, have you considered that you shouldn't do it?"

She didn't speak, just nuzzled back into the embrace. It wasn't an option. She knew that, and he did, too. Her work and the length of her contracts hadn't been a secret, after all. From the first week they had met, the clock had been counting down on their time together, and both of them had been well aware of it. *If only I'd known what a good hugger he is, I wouldn't have had to miss out on this for all these months*, she thought with regret. But more contact with Enes, any more depth to their relationship...it would only have made this harder. And it was already hard enough.

She let the hug continue a moment longer, then stepped back, breaking the connection. "Thanks," she said, forcing a smile and willing her eyes to stop leaking tears. "I'll let you know soon about the trip to Germany. I'm sure Badem will be more than happy to stay with you."

Enes just nodded, his smile sympathetic as Celia gave him a wave and retreated down the stairs to her apartment.

Sixteen

It was only a week later that everything fell into place for Celia's trip to Germany.

"Okay," she told Enes, as she dropped off Badem in her cat carrier. "I'm leaving in the morning, early. So it only makes sense to leave her with you tonight, so I don't have to wake you up tomorrow—"

"I wouldn't mind," he interjected. "For what it's worth."

She smiled at him. "And I appreciate that. I appreciate you for"—she gestured vaguely around them—"all of this. It's such a relief not to have to worry about Badem when I'm gone. I know it's going to be a short trip, and I probably could have just left enough food and water and clean litter for her and it all would have been fine..." She trailed off.

Enes nodded. "Sure, but if you were worried the whole time, then that would hardly be a good plan."

"Right. And I would have been. Plus, what if my flight back was delayed?" She shook her head. "No, this is the way to go. And I am so grateful to you for it."

"You may have already mentioned that." But Enes was smiling, looking at her with affection. He tipped his head towards Badem. "So, what else do we need? Let me come downstairs to pick up her litter box and whatever else there is."

The two of them took another trip down and up the stairs together, bringing all of Badem's things. For such a small animal, she needed a disproportionate amount of luggage.

"All set then," Celia said, brushing her hands on her thighs. "Thanks, again."

Enes shook his head, then pulled her in for a quick hug. "Don't mention it. Just come back home safely, okay?"

Celia nodded. Home. It all felt like home. Istanbul. Her apartment. Badem. Enes. This moment felt like she was leaving home for the first time since she had boarded a one-way flight from St. Louis, and she was already aching to return. *Just a few days*, she reminded herself. She would be working remotely on her Aslanbey Holding contract, while simultaneously doing site visits and a few brief meetings at the two potential companies she was considering for her next contract. It was bound to be a busy time, and she was sure—or almost sure, at least—that she wouldn't even have a moment to miss Badem or Enes.

Her apartment felt strangely empty without Badem's presence. Celia finished packing her small carryon bag, busying herself cleaning up the kitchen and adding a few steps to her nighttime skincare routine.

But it hadn't been enough to distract her from the gaping hole in her life, in her heart. There was no Badem underfoot, tangling in her legs and nearly tripping her as she hurried through the apartment. There were no chirps, no meows, no purrs in the cavernously silent space. It all felt a little too much like life before Badem, and Celia hadn't realized, not until that moment, just how empty that life had been. A luxury apartment in an interesting city, cat hair-free clothes that were flattering and professional, evenings of working away on the couch while sipping a local wine. It all sounded good—hell, it all felt good, at least in the short term—but she didn't want it anymore.

Not that what she wanted mattered. This was the life she had signed up for, and it was a good life. Celia forcefully flicked off the light switch and then flopped onto her bed gracelessly. No need to be careful about not squishing a cat paw when the spot next to her on the bed was vacant.

It was that vacant spot that kept her awake at first. Celia had gotten used to the comforting presence of her small, furry, purring companion, that was no surprise. But without it, her mind took over, running rampant with thoughts she had been suppressing for weeks.

I don't want this anymore, she admitted to herself. *I'm tired, and God, the thought of leaving makes me so sad. So why do I insist that it's the only option? Is it really?* But a solution didn't present itself. It wasn't that easy, Celia knew. If people could just live where they wanted to live and work where they wanted to work, things like immigration and taxes wouldn't be as complicated as they were.

She let herself despair, telling herself it would be just a moment of self-pity and then she would get back to normal. But the tears started, and they didn't stop. The sadness she felt at leaving Badem and Enes ran deep. It wasn't that she couldn't bear to be apart from her cat for a few days…it was the symbolism of it and what she feared it meant on a deeper level. It was a taste of what the future held. Because even though a big part of her refused to admit the truth, a small rational voice in her head was telling her this was the way it had to be. Celia moving on for the next job, Badem staying with Enes. It was unfair to the cat to subject her to a life of international moves every six months, and she knew Enes would take good care of her.

She heard the sound of footsteps moving upstairs in Enes's apartment, and her tears flowed even more freely. When she was gone, she wouldn't hear that sound again. She would hear new neighbors, unfamiliar ones. People she might never meet. Certainly not a handsome vet who would become one of her favorite people, a built-in companion for all of her favorite evenings.

That thought flipped a switch in her mind, stopping the tears. She didn't want to start over with new people. And why should she, when she had found something so special here? All those evenings curled up on the couch with Badem, Enes next to them, chatting about their days and laughing at the antics of the characters on the screen…that felt like home. Family. And it didn't matter if she and Enes weren't a couple, if things between them never progressed beyond friendship. Wasn't a friendship like theirs worth preserving? Worth treasuring? She wasn't naïve enough to think she would find the same thing everywhere she went, and the evidence from her past decade of country hopping supported that opinion. There were great people everywhere. Terrible people everywhere, too. But the soul connections, the friends who fit into your life like they were meant to be there? Those were the rarest of gems, and they deserved to be treasured as such.

And with that thought, Celia knew what she had to do. She fumbled on the bedside table for her phone, fired off a few emails, and fell asleep with a smile on her face and resolve in her heart.

Seventeen

Ayla met Celia early the next morning at a cafe near the Aslanbey Holding office. "Thanks for coming so early," said Celia with an apologetic smile. "I'm sorry to drag you out of bed at such an unpleasant hour."

"Don't worry about it." Ayla waved a dismissive hand. "What are friends for?"

Celia smiled. That's right, Ayla was her friend, too. It wasn't just Badem and Enes she had found in Istanbul. It was also Ayla and Meryem and even Kemal. She had encountered kindness at every turn, and she had barely scratched the surface of what the city had to offer.

So far, at least. So far, she had barely scratched the surface, but...

"So, why are we meeting here?" Ayla asked, gesturing around them. "It's a nice cafe, but we could have just talked at work like normal, you know."

"I'm not coming in today. Working from home. Well, actually, I'm supposed to be working from the road, but I canceled my trip to Germany—"

"You..." Ayla looked shocked. "What? Why? I mean, why were you going to Germany, and why are you not now?"

"The plan was to scope out a few companies, figure out where my next contract is going to be."

"Ah." Ayla's expression fell, but she forced a smile. "That's nice. I've heard good things about Germany."

"Right," Celia continued. "But I canceled the trip because...well, because I want to stay here."

Ayla's mouth dropped open, her eyes widening at the same time, the final effect looking almost exactly like the shocked emoji.

"You...really?" When Celia nodded, Ayla grinned. "That's amazing. I...what can I do to help?"

Celia smiled back at her friend. "I'm so glad you asked that. You said something before about someone you know going through the residence permit process?"

Eighteen

Celia's fingers trembled as she knocked on Enes's door that evening. He was going to be surprised to see her, there was no doubt about that.

But would he be happy about her news? Disappointed he wouldn't get to keep Badem for himself? Or worst of all, indifferent?

There was only one way to find out.

She was steeling herself when the door flung open, Enes's face full of concern.

"Celia? Is everything okay?" His eyes were traveling over her body as if checking to ensure she hadn't been injured. "Did you miss your flight? Do you need a ride to the airport?"

That got a laugh out of Celia. "Considering that my flight was at eight o'clock this morning, yes. I'd say I missed it. But it's okay. I did it on purpose."

"You…" He stepped aside, gesturing for her to come inside. "Come in, talk to me. I don't think I'm understanding what you're saying."

Celia followed him inside, into his living room that was so similar to her own. And there, just one floor up from her normal perch, was Badem, her legs tucked under her in a neat little loaf on the couch. On Celia's approach, she gave one sharp meow, got to her feet, and bounded in her direction.

Celia crouched down to scratch the top of Badem's head, rewarded immediately by the sound of her familiar purr. She felt herself grinning at this animal that had so quickly endeared herself, had burrowed so deeply into Celia's heart.

She looked up to find Enes watching the two of them, his smile full of warmth and affection. He gestured to the couch. "Will you sit? Can I make you some tea?"

Celia nodded. "That would be great, thanks."

While Enes was preparing tea for the two of them, Celia got comfortable on his couch, with Badem immediately claiming her spot on Celia's lap.

"So what happened with your trip?" Enes asked from the kitchen, just a few feet away. It was an open living area, and he clearly didn't care to wait to continue their conversation until they were both seated.

"I'm not going," said Celia.

"Right." Enes nodded. "I figured that. Are you going to take the trip later? Or...I don't know, do virtual meetings instead? I can watch Badem anytime you want me to. She was a great little houseguest last night. Does she—"

"No, Enes." Celia interrupted him. "I mean, I'm not going to Germany. I'm staying."

He turned slowly to face her, his eyes uncomprehending. "What do you mean?"

Celia shrugged. "I mean that I'm not done here. I want to stay."

He approached her slowly, as if she were a wild animal and he didn't want to scare her away. "I...you...what?" Finally close enough, he sat down next to her, his eyes still fixed on hers. "Really?"

Celia felt her eyes brimming with tears at something she saw on his face. There was surprise, yes. But more than that, she saw joy. Relief. Hope. "Really. I like being here, with you and with Badem. I don't want to leave her. And I don't want to leave Istanbul."

"Of course." Enes nodded. "Of course. Well, what can I do? Do you want me to help you search for a new job? See if I have any connections that might have a vacancy?"

She quirked an eyebrow at him. "You mean you think one of your vet school classmates might need an efficiency consultant for their practice?"

"I don't know...maybe?" Enes shrugged. "But it's a big city, Celia. I'm sure we can find something."

She put her hand over his and gave it a squeeze. "It's okay, Enes. I got some great news today. My friend Ayla connected me with her cousin's girlfriend, who just went through the residence permit process." She shrugged. "It turns out it's a pretty straightforward process, especially if you're already established. I can keep working for myself, keep doing the work that I love."

"And there are plenty of businesses in Istanbul for you to consult with?" Enes asked, a hint of hesitation in his voice. "You won't run out of potential contracts soon, will you?"

Celia chuckled. "Lucky for you, you live in one of the largest cities in the world. If you were in a tiny village or on an island somewhere, this might never have worked."

"I...me?" Enes shook his head. "You're not staying for me, are you? I...that..."

"No." Celia's tone was decisive, confident. "I'm staying for me. I'm ready to live somewhere, not just be a long-term visitor. And this feels like the place for me to do that."

"I see." Enes's expression had dropped, but he raised the corners of his mouth in a smile again. "Well, I'm glad you're going to be around, no matter what."

"And of course I do still want to be near you, Enes. You and Badem are, like...well, it probably sounds stupid, but you're like my family. I've never had someone to come home to like I have with the two of you these last few months, and..." She shrugged, feeling sheepish. "It's been really nice."

He reached for her hand, pulling her closer. "I..." When words failed him, his hands came up to her jaw, his eyes searching hers with a question. As she nodded back, his face was already moving closer, his mouth coming to meet hers. The connection was electric, a bolt of sensation traveling from the base of Celia's spine all the way up and blasting out of the crown of her head. When she finally pulled back to catch her breath, her lips were still tingling.

Enes's pupils were blown, his breathing as heavy as hers. "That's been a long time coming," he admitted.

"Really?" Celia felt the lingering heat on her cheeks, her heart still beating a tattoo. "I thought..."

Enes huffed out a laugh. "You thought I spent every evening with you because I *wasn't* interested?"

"No, I just...well, yes. I thought we were great friends and you wouldn't want to mess that up."

Enes shook his head. "I love being your friend. But I believe we could be more than that, too. I just didn't want to complicate things when you were planning to leave."

"Really?"

He nodded. "I didn't want to make the decision harder for you...and I didn't want to make it even more difficult for me to say goodbye to you, either." He took her hands in his, giving them a squeeze. "But you're really staying, right?"

Celia nodded. "I'm really staying."

His grin was a beautiful sight. "Then I can't wait to see what the two of us can become."

Badem got to her feet then, rubbing the corner of her mouth on their interlocked hands.

Celia chuckled at the cat. "I think you mean what the *three* of us can become."

She released Enes's hands then, pulling him closer by his collar and bringing their lips together. She felt his smile against hers before losing herself in the heat of him, the taste of him. And she knew then, that she was home.

On the far corner of the couch, Badem closed her eyes, purring happily. She was home, too.

Author's Note

One of my favorite things about living in Turkey is the cats. Badem was inspired by our own cats and the experiences we have shared, and there is a constant flow of inspiration for more stories. Most of the characteristics of Badem come from our Angie, who was originally called Badem by the neighbor who fed her as a kitten. One of my favorite moments though, where she climbs down the tree backwards, was inspired by our Sis, who did the same thing after treeing herself far higher than we would have been able to rescue her.

To stay updated on other works in progress or purchase books and bundles directly from me, please visit my website at kcmccormickciftci.com.

If you loved this book, please consider leaving a review, as that is one of the best ways to support indie authors like me. Reviews left on major retail sites (wherever you bought this book is a great start!), Goodreads, and Book-Bub will help other readers discover this book, too.

About the Author

KC McCormick Çiftçi is an English teacher turned romance writer. She spent the majority of her twenties living and working abroad, collecting the experiences that inform the stories she tells. She enjoys telling multicultural and international love stories through romantic comedy and women's fiction. She lives in Turkey with her husband and a herd of cats.

Prior to diving into the world of romance, KC published two self-help books for intercultural couples, *Loving Across Borders* and *The K-1 Visa Wedding Plan*. Both are available wherever books are sold.

For updates on upcoming releases, behind the scenes news, and all my favorite book recommendations, visit kcmccormickciftci.com (or just point your phone camera at the QR code below).

Books by KC McCormick Çiftçi

Austen in Turkey

Pride, Prejudice, & Turkish Delight

Sense, Sensibility, & the Mediterranean Sea

Home (Abroad) for the Holidays

Christmas on Inishmore

Christmas at Terminal One

Intoxicated by You

Intoxicated by You

Cats of Istanbul

The Vet Upstairs

Intercultural Relationship Self Help

Loving Across Borders

The K-1 Visa Wedding Plan